Friedrich de la Motte Fouque

Sintram and his Companions

Outlook

Friedrich de la Motte Fouque

Sintram and his Companions

1. Auflage | ISBN: 978-3-73261-952-8

Erscheinungsort: Paderborn, Deutschland

Erscheinungsjahr: 2018

Outlook Verlag GmbH, Paderborn.

Sintram and His Companions

by Friedrich de la Motte Fouque

with foreword by Charlotte M Yonge.

Introduction

Four tales are, it is said, intended by the Author to be appropriate to the Four Seasons: the stern, grave "Sintram", to winter; the tearful, smiling, fresh "Undine", to Spring; the torrid deserts of the "Two Captains", to summer; and the sunset gold of "Aslauga's Knight", to autumn. Of these two are before us.

The author of these tales, as well as of many more, was Friedrich, Baron de la Motte Fouque, one of the foremost of the minstrels or tale-tellers of the realm of spiritual chivalry—the realm whither Arthur's knights departed when they "took the Sancgreal's holy quest,"—whence Spenser's Red Cross knight and his fellows came forth on their adventures, and in which the Knight of la Mancha believed, and endeavoured to exist.

La Motte Fouque derived his name and his title from the French Huguenot ancestry, who had fled on the Revocation of the Edict of Nantes. His Christian name was taken from his godfather, Frederick the Great, of whom his father was a faithful friend, without compromising his religious principles and practice. Friedrich was born at Brandenburg on February 12, 1777, was educated by good parents at home, served in the Prussian army through disaster and success, took an enthusiastic part in the rising of his country against Napoleon, inditing as many battle-songs as Korner. When victory was achieved, he dedicated his sword in the church of Neunhausen where his estate lay. He lived there, with his beloved wife and his imagination, till his death in 1843.

And all the time life was to him a poet's dream. He lived in a continual glamour of spiritual romance, bathing everything, from the old deities of the Valhalla down to the champions of German liberation, in an ideal glow of purity and nobleness, earnestly Christian throughout, even in his dealings with Northern mythology, for he saw Christ unconsciously shown in Baldur, and Satan in Loki.

Thus he lived, felt, and believed what he wrote, and though his dramas and poems do not rise above fair mediocrity, and the great number of his prose stories are injured by a certain monotony, the charm of them is in their elevation of sentiment and the earnest faith pervading all. His knights might be Sir Galahad—

"My strength is as the strength of ten,
Because my heart is pure."

Evil comes to them as something to be conquered, generally as a form of magic enchantment, and his "wondrous fair maidens" are worthy of them. Yet there is adventure enough to afford much pleasure, and often we have a touch of true genius, which has given actual ideas to the world, and precious ones.

This genius is especially traceable in his two masterpieces, Sintram and Undine. Sintram was inspired by Albert Durer's engraving of the "Knight of Death," of which we give a presentation. It was sent to Fouque by his friend Edward Hitzig, with a request that he would compose a ballad on it. The date of the engraving is 1513, and we quote the description given by the late Rev. R. St. John Tyrwhitt, showing how differently it may be read.

The Knight, Death, and Satan.
(Albert Dürer.)

"Some say it is the end of the strong wicked man, just overtaken by Death and Sin, whom he has served on earth. It is said that the tuft on the lance indicates his murderous character, being of such unusual size. You know the use of that appendage was to prevent blood running down from the spearhead to the hands. They also think that the object under the horse's off hind foot is a snare, into which the old oppressor is to fall instantly. The expression of the faces may be taken either way: both good men and bad may have hard, regular features; and both good men and bad would set their teeth grimly on seeing Death, with the sands of their life nearly run out. Some say they think the expression of Death gentle, or only admonitory (as the author of "Sintram"); and I have to thank the authoress of the "Heir of Redclyffe" for showing me a fine impression of the plate, where Death certainly had a not ungentle countenance—snakes and all. I think the shouldered lance, and quiet, firm seat on horseback, with gentle bearing on the curb-bit, indicate grave resolution in the rider, and that a robber knight would have his lance in rest; then there is the leafy crown on the horse's head; and the horse and dog move on so quietly, that I am inclined to hope the best for the Ritter."

Musing on the mysterious engraving, Fouque saw in it the life-long companions of man, Death and Sin, whom he must defy in order to reach salvation; and out of that contemplation rose his wonderful romance, not exactly an allegory, where every circumstance can be fitted with an appropriate meaning, but with the sense of the struggle of life, with external temptation and hereditary inclination pervading all, while Grace and Prayer aid the effort. Folko and Gabrielle are revived from the Magic Ring, that Folko may by example and influence enhance all higher resolutions; while Gabrielle, in all unconscious innocence, awakes the passions, and thus makes the conquest the harder.

It is within the bounds of possibility that the similarities of folk- lore may have brought to Fouque's knowledge the outline of the story which Scott tells us was the germ of "Guy Mannering"; where a boy, whose horoscope had been drawn by an astrologer, as likely to encounter peculiar trials at certain intervals, actually had, in his twenty-first year, a sort of visible encounter with the Tempter, and came off conqueror by his strong faith in the Bible. Sir Walter, between reverence and realism, only took the earlier part of the story, but Fouque gives us the positive struggle, and carries us along with the final victory and subsequent peace. His tale has had a remarkable power over the readers. We cannot but mention two remarkable instances at either end of the scale. Cardinal Newman, in his younger days, was so much overcome by it that he hurried out into the garden to read it alone, and returned with traces of emotion in his face. And when Charles Lowder read it to his East End boys, their whole minds seemed engrossed by it, and they even called certain spots after the places mentioned. Imagine the Rocks of the Moon in Ratcliff Highway!

May we mention that Miss Christabel Coleridge's "Waynflete" brings something of the spirit and idea of "Sintram" into modern life?

"Undine" is a story of much lighter fancy, and full of a peculiar grace, though with a depth of melancholy that endears it. No doubt it was founded on the universal idea in folk-lore of the nixies or water-spirits, one of whom, in Norwegian legend, was seen weeping bitterly because of the want of a soul.

4

Sometimes the nymph is a wicked siren like the Lorelei; but in many of these tales she weds an earthly lover, and deserts him after a time, sometimes on finding her diving cap, or her seal-skin garment, which restores her to her ocean kindred, sometimes on his intruding on her while she is under a periodical transformation, as with the fairy Melusine, more rarely if he becomes unfaithful.

There is a remarkable Cornish tale of a nymph or mermaiden, who thus vanished, leaving a daughter who loved to linger on the beach rather than sport with other children. By and by she had a lover, but no sooner did he show tokens of inconstancy, than the mother came up from the sea and put him to death, when the daughter pined away and died. Her name was Selina, which gives the tale a modern aspect, and makes us wonder if the old tradition can have been modified by some report of Undine's story.

There was an idea set forth by the Rosicrucians of spirits abiding in the elements, and as Undine represented the water influences, Fouque's wife, the Baroness Caroline, wrote a fairly pretty story on the sylphs of fire. But Undine's freakish playfulness and mischief as an elemental being, and her sweet patience when her soul is won, are quite original, and indeed we cannot help sharing, or at least understanding, Huldbrand's beginning to shrink from the unearthly creature to something of his own flesh and blood. He is altogether unworthy, and though in this tale there is far less of spiritual meaning than in Sintram, we cannot but see that Fouque's thought was that the grosser human nature is unable to appreciate what is absolutely pure and unearthly.

C. M. YONGE.

CHAPTER 1

In the high castle of Drontheim many knights sat assembled to hold council for the weal of the realm; and joyously they caroused together till midnight around the huge stone table in the vaulted hall. A rising storm drove the snow wildly against the rattling windows; all the oak doors groaned, the massive locks shook, the castle-clock slowly and heavily struck the hour of one. Then a boy, pale as death, with disordered hair and closed eyes, rushed into the hall, uttering a wild scream of terror. He stopped beside the richly carved seat of the mighty Biorn, clung to the glittering knight with both his hands, and shrieked in a piercing voice, "Knight and father! father and knight! Death and another are closely pursuing me!"

An awful stillness lay like ice on the whole assembly, save that the boy screamed ever the fearful words. But one of Biorn's numerous retainers, an old esquire, known by the name of Rolf the Good, advanced towards the terrified child, took him in his arms, and half chanted this prayer: "O Father, help Thy servant! I believe, and yet I cannot believe." The boy, as if in a dream, at once loosened his hold of the knight; and the good Rolf bore him from the hall unresisting, yet still shedding hot tears and murmuring confused sounds.

The lords and knights looked at one another much amazed, until the mighty Biorn said, wildly and fiercely laughing, "Marvel not at that strange boy. He is my only son; and has been thus since he was five years old: he is now twelve. I am therefore accustomed to see him so; though, at the first, I too was disquieted by it. The attack comes upon him only once in the year, and always at this same time. But forgive me for having spent so many words on my poor Sintram, and let us pass on to some worthier subject for our discourse."

Again there was silence for a while; then whisperingly and doubtfully single voices strove to renew their broken-off discourse, but without success. Two of the youngest and most joyous began a roundelay; but the storm howled and raged so wildly without, that this too was soon interrupted. And now they all sat silent and motionless in the lofty hall; the lamp flickered sadly under the vaulted roof; the whole party of knights looked like pale, lifeless images dressed up in gigantic armour.

Then arose the chaplain of the castle of Drontheim, the only priest among the knightly throng, and said, "Dear Lord Biorn, our eyes and thoughts have all been directed to you and your son in a wonderful manner; but so it has been ordered by the providence of God. You perceive that we cannot withdraw them; and you would do well to tell us exactly what you know concerning the fearful state of the boy. Perchance, the solemn tale, which I expect from you, might do good to this disturbed assembly."

Biorn cast a look of displeasure on the priest, and answered, "Sir chaplain, you have more share in the history than either you or I could desire. Excuse me, if I am unwilling to trouble these light- hearted warriors with so rueful a tale."

But the chaplain approached nearer to the knight, and said, in a firm yet very mild tone, "Dear lord, hitherto it rested with you alone to relate, or not to relate it; but now that you have so strangely hinted at the share which I have had in your son's calamity, I must positively demand that you will repeat word for word how everything came to pass. My honour will have it so, and that will weigh with you as much as with me."

In stern compliance Biorn bowed his haughty head, and began the following narration. "This time seven years I was keeping the Christmas feast with my assembled followers. We have many venerable old customs which have descended to us by inheritance from our great forefathers; as, for instance, that of placing a gilded boar's head on the table, and making thereon knightly vows of daring and wondrous deeds. Our chaplain here, who used then frequently to visit me, was never a friend to keeping up such traditions of the ancient heathen world. Such men as he were not much in favour in those olden times."

"My excellent predecessors," interrupted the chaplain, "belonged more to God than to the world, and with Him they were in favour. Thus they converted your ancestors; and if I can in like manner be of service to you, even your jeering will not vex me."

With looks yet darker, and a somewhat angry shudder, the knight resumed: "Yes, yes; I know all your promises and threats of an invisible Power, and how they are meant persuade us to part more readily with whatever of this world's goods we may possess. Once, ah, truly, once I too had such! Strange!
—Sometimes it seems to me as though ages had passed over since then, and as if I were alone the survivor, so fearfully has everything changed. But now I bethink me, that the greater part of this noble company knew me in my happiness, and have seen my wife, my lovely Verena."

He pressed his hands on his eyes, and it seemed as though he wept. The storm had ceased; the soft light of the moon shone through the windows, and her beams played on his wild features. Suddenly he started up, so that his heavy armour rattled with a fearful sound, and he cried out in a thundering voice, "Shall I turn monk, as she has become a nun? No, crafty priest; your webs are too thin to catch flies of my sort."

"I have nothing to do with webs," said the chaplain. "In all openness and sincerity have I put heaven and hell before you during the space of six years; and you gave full consent to the step which the holy Verena took. But what all that has to do with your son's sufferings I know not, and I wait for your narration."

7

"You may wait long enough," said Biorn, with a sneer. "Sooner shall—"

"Swear not!" said the chaplain in a loud commanding tone, and his eyes flashed almost fearfully.

"Hurra!" cried Biorn, in wild affright; "hurra! Death and his companion are loose!" and he dashed madly out of the chamber and down the steps. The rough and fearful notes of his horn were heard summoning his retainers; and presently afterwards the clatter of horses' feet on the frozen court-yard gave token of their departure. The knights retired, silent and shuddering; while the chaplain remained alone at the huge stone table, praying.

CHAPTER 2

After some time the good Rolf returned with slow and soft steps, and started with surprise at finding the hall deserted. The chamber where he had been occupied in quieting and soothing the unhappy child was in so distant a part of the castle that he had heard nothing of the knight's hasty departure. The chaplain related to him all that had passed, and then said, "But, my good Rolf, I much wish to ask you concerning those strange words with which you seemed to lull poor Sintram to rest. They sounded like sacred words, and no doubt they are; but I could not understand them. 'I believe, and yet I cannot believe.'"

"Reverend sir," answered Rolf, "I remember that from my earliest years no history in the Gospels has taken such hold of me as that of the child possessed with a devil, which the disciples were not able to cast out; but when our Saviour came down from the mountain where He had been transfigured, He broke the bonds wherewith the evil spirit had held the miserable child bound. I always felt as if I must have known and loved that boy, and been his play- fellow in his happy days; and when I grew older, then the distress of the father on account of his lunatic son lay heavy at my heart. It must surely have all been a foreboding of our poor young Lord Sintram, whom I love as if he were my own child; and now the words of the weeping father in the Gospel often come into my mind,—'Lord, I believe; help Thou my unbelief;' and something similar I may very likely have repeated to-day as a chant or a prayer. Reverend father, when I consider how one dreadful imprecation of the father has kept its withering hold on the son, all seems dark before me; but, God be praised! my faith and my hope remain above."

"Good Rolf," said the priest, "I cannot clearly understand what you say about the unhappy Sintram; for I do not know when and how this affliction came upon him. If no oath or solemn promise bind you to secrecy, will you make known to me all that is connected with it?"

"Most willingly," replied Rolf. "I have long desired to have an opportunity of so doing; but you have been almost always separated from us. I dare not now leave the sleeping boy any longer alone; and to-morrow, at the earliest dawn, I must take him to his father. Will you come with me, dear sir, to our poor Sintram?"

The chaplain at once took up the small lamp which Rolf had brought with him, and they set off together through the long vaulted passages. In the small distant chamber they found the poor boy fast asleep. The light of the lamp fell strangely on his very pale face. The chaplain stood gazing at him for some time, and at length said: "Certainly from his birth his features were always sharp and strongly marked, but now they are almost fearfully so for such a child; and yet no one can help having a kindly feeling towards him, whether he will or not."

"Most true, dear sir," answered Rolf. And it was evident how his whole heart rejoiced at any word which betokened affection for his beloved young lord. Thereupon he placed the lamp where its light could not disturb the boy, and seating himself close by the priest, he began to speak in the following terms:— "During that Christmas feast of which my lord was talking to you, he and his followers discoursed much concerning the German merchants, and the best means of keeping down the increasing pride and power of the trading- towns. At length Biorn laid his impious hand on the golden boar's head, and swore to put to death without mercy every German trader whom fate, in what way soever, might bring alive into his power. The gentle Verena turned pale, and would have interposed—but it was too late, the bloody word was uttered. And immediately afterwards, as though the great enemy of souls were determined at once to secure with fresh bonds the vassal thus devoted to him, a warder came into the hall to announce that two citizens of a trading-town in Germany, an old man and his son, had been shipwrecked on this coast, and were now within the gates, asking hospitality of the lord of the castle. The knight could not refrain from shuddering; but he thought himself bound by his rash vow and by that accursed heathenish golden boar. We, his retainers, were commanded to assemble in the castle-yard, armed with sharp spears, which were to be hurled at the defenceless strangers at the first signal made to us. For the first, and I trust the last time in my life, I said 'No' to the commands of my lord; and that I said in a loud voice, and with the heartiest determination. The Almighty, who alone knows whom He will accept and whom He will reject, armed me with resolution and strength. And Biorn might perceive whence the refusal of his faithful old servant arose, and that it was worthy of respect. He said to me, half in anger and half in scorn: 'Go up to my wife's apartments; her attendants are running to and fro, perhaps she is ill. Go up, Rolf the Good, I say to thee, and so women shall be with women.' I thought to myself, 'Jeer on, then;' and I went silently the way that he had pointed out to me. On the stairs there met me two strange and right fearful beings, whom I had never seen before; and I know not how they got into the castle. One of them was a great tall man, frightfully pallid and thin; the other was a dwarf-like man, with a most hideous countenance and features. Indeed, when I collected my thoughts and looked carefully at him, it appeared to me —"

Low moanings and convulsive movements of the boy here interrupted the narrative. Rolf and his chaplain hastened to his bedside, and perceived that his countenance wore an expression of fearful agony, and that he was struggling in vain to open his eyes. The priest made the Sign of the Cross over him, and immediately peace seemed to be restored, and his sleep again became quiet: they both returned softly to their seats.

"You see," said Rolf, "that it will not do to describe more closely those two awful beings. Suffice it to say, that they went down into the court-yard, and that I proceeded to my lady's apartments. I found the gentle Verena almost fainting with terror and overwhelming anxiety, and I hastened to restore her with some of those remedies which I was able to apply by my skill, through God's gift and the healing virtues of herbs and minerals. But scarcely had she recovered her senses, when, with that calm holy power which, as you know, is hers, she desired me to conduct her down to the court-yard, saying that she must either put a stop to the fearful doings of this night, or herself fall a sacrifice. Our way took us by the little bed of the sleeping Sintram. Alas! hot tears fell from my eyes to see how evenly his gentle breath then came and went, and how sweetly he smiled in his peaceful slumbers."

The old man put his hands to his eyes, and wept bitterly; but soon he resumed his sad story. "As we approached the lowest window of the staircase, we could hear distinctly the voice of the elder merchant; and on looking out, the light of the torches showed me his noble features, as well as the bright youthful countenance of his son. 'I take Almighty God to witness,' cried he, 'that I had no evil thought against this house! But surely I must have fallen unawares amongst heathens; it cannot be that I am in a Christian knight's castle; and if you are indeed heathens, then kill us at once. And thou, my beloved son, be patient and of good courage; in heaven we shall learn wherefore it could not be otherwise.' I thought I could see those two fearful ones amidst the throng of retainers. The pale one had a huge curved sword in his hand, the little one held a spear notched in a strange fashion. Verena tore open the window, and cried in silvery tones through the wild night, 'My dearest lord and husband, for the sake of your only child, have pity on those harmless men! Save them from death, and resist the temptation of the evil spirit.' The knight answered in his fierce wrath—but I cannot repeat his words. He staked his child on the desperate cast; he called Death and the Devil to see that he kept his word:—but hush! the boy is again moaning. Let me bring the dark tale quickly to a close. Biorn commanded his followers to strike, casting on them those fierce looks which have gained him the title of Biorn of the Fiery Eyes; while at the same time the two frightful strangers bestirred themselves very busily. Then Verena called out, with piercing anguish, 'Help, O God, my Saviour!' Those two dreadful figures disappeared; and the knight and his retainers, as if seized with blindness, rushed wildly one against the other, but without doing injury to themselves, or yet being able to strike the merchants, who ran so close a risk. They bowed reverently towards Verena, and with calm thanksgivings departed through the castle- gates, which at that moment had been burst open by a violent gust of wind, and now gave a free passage to any who would go forth. The lady and I were yet standing bewildered on the stairs, when I fancied I saw the two fearful forms glide close by me, but mist-like and unreal. Verena called to me: 'Rolf, did you see a tall pale man, and a little hideous one with him, pass just now up the staircase?' I flew after them; and found, alas, the poor boy in the same state in which you saw him a few hours ago. Ever since, the attack has come on him regularly at this time, and he is in all respects fearfully changed. The lady of the castle did not fail to discern the avenging hand of Heaven in this calamity; and as the knight, her husband, instead of repenting, ever became more truly Biorn of the Fiery Eyes, she resolved, in the walls of a cloister, by unremitting prayer, to obtain mercy in time and eternity for herself and her unhappy child."

Rolf was silent; and the chaplain, after some thought, said: "I now understand why, six years ago, Biorn confessed his guilt to me in general words, and consented that his wife should take the veil. Some faint compunction must then have stirred within him, and perhaps may stir him yet. At any rate it was impossible that so tender a flower as Verena could remain longer in so rough keeping. But who is there now to watch over and protect our poor Sintram?"

"The prayer of his mother," answered Rolf. "Reverend sir, when the first dawn of day appears, as it does now, and when the morning breeze whispers through the glancing window, they ever bring to my mind the soft beaming eyes of my lady, and I again seem to hear the sweet tones of her voice. The holy Verena is, next to God, our chief aid."

"And let us add our devout supplications to the Lord," said the chaplain; and he and Rolf knelt in silent and earnest prayer by the bed of the pale sufferer, who began to smile in his dreams.

CHAPTER 3

The rays of the sun shining brightly into the room awoke Sintram, and raising himself up, he looked angrily at the chaplain, and said, "So there is a priest in the castle! And yet that accursed dream continues to torment me even in his very presence. Pretty priest he must be!"

"My child," answered the chaplain in the mildest tone, "I have prayed for thee most fervently, and I shall never cease doing so—but God alone is Almighty."

"You speak very boldly to the son of the knight Biorn," cried Sintram. "'My child!' If those horrible dreams had not been again haunting me, you would make me laugh heartily."

"Young Lord Sintram," said the chaplain, "I am by no means surprised that you do not know me again; for in truth, neither do I know you again." And his eyes filled with tears as he spoke.

The good Rolf looked sorrowfully in the boy's face, saying, "Ah, my dear young master, you are so much better than you would make people believe. Why do you that? Your memory is so good, that you must surely recollect your kind old friend the chaplain, who used formerly to be constantly at the castle, and to bring you so many gifts— bright pictures of saints, and beautiful songs?"

"I know all that very well," replied Sintram thoughtfully. "My sainted mother was alive in those days."

"Our gracious lady is still living, God be praised," said the good Rolf.

"But she does not live for us, poor sick creatures that we are!" cried Sintram. "And why will you not call her sainted? Surely she knows nothing about my dreams?"

"Yes, she does know of them," said the chaplain; "and she prays to God for you. But take heed, and restrain that wild, haughty temper of yours. It might, indeed, come to pass that she would know nothing about your dreams, and that would be if your soul were separated from your body; and then the holy angels also would cease to know anything of you."

Sintram fell back on his bed as if thunderstruck; and Rolf said, with a gentle sigh, "You should not speak so severely to my poor sick child, reverend sir."

The boy sat up, and with tearful eyes he turned caressingly towards the chaplain: "Let him do as he pleases, you good, tender-hearted Rolf; he knows very well what he is about. Would you reprove him if I were slipping down a snow-cleft, and he caught me up roughly by the hair of my head?"

The priest looked tenderly at him, and would have spoken his holy thoughts, when Sintram suddenly sprang off the bed and asked after his father. As soon as he heard of the knight's departure, he would not remain another hour in the castle; and put aside the fears of the chaplain and the old esquire, lest a rapid journey should injure his hardly restored health, by saying to them, "Believe me, reverend sir, and dear old Rolf, if I were not subject to these hideous dreams, there would not be a bolder youth in the whole world; and even as it is, I am not so far behind the very best. Besides, till another year has passed, my dreams are at an end."

On his somewhat imperious sign Rolf brought out the horses. The boy threw himself boldly into the saddle, and taking a courteous leave of the chaplain, he dashed along the frozen valley that lay between the snow-clad mountains. He had not ridden far, in company with his old attendant, when he heard a strange indistinct sound proceeding from a neighbouring cleft in the rock; it was partly like the clapper of a small mill, but mingled with that were hollow groans and other tones of distress. Thither they turned their horses, and a wonderful sight showed itself to them.

A tall man, deadly pale, in a pilgrim's garb, was striving with violent though unsuccessful efforts, to work his way out of the snow and to climb up the mountain; and thereby a quantity of bones, which were hanging loosely all about his garments, rattled one against the other, and caused the mysterious sound already mentioned. Rolf, much terrified, crossed himself, while the bold Sintram called out to the stranger, "What art thou doing there? Give an account of thy solitary labours."

"I live in death," replied that other one with a fearful grin.

"Whose are those bones on thy clothes?"

"They are relics, young sir."

"Art thou a pilgrim?"

"Restless, quietless, I wander up and down."

"Thou must not perish here in the snow before my eyes."

"That I will not."

"Thou must come up and sit on my horse."

"That I will." And all at once he started up out of the snow with surprising strength and agility, and sat on the horse behind Sintram, clasping him tight in his long arms. The horse, startled by the rattling of the bones, and as if seized with madness, rushed away through the most trackless passes. The boy soon found himself alone with his strange companion; for Rolf, breathless with fear, spurred on his horse in vain, and remained far behind them. From a snowy precipice the horse slid, without falling, into a narrow gorge, somewhat indeed exhausted, yet continuing to snort and foam as before, and still unmastered by the boy. Yet his headlong course being now changed into a rough irregular trot, Sintram was able to breathe more freely, and to begin the following discourse with his unknown companion.

"Draw thy garment closer around thee, thou pale man, so the bones will not rattle, and I shall be able to curb my horse."

"It would be of no avail, boy; it would be of no avail. The bones must rattle."

"Do not clasp me so tight with thy long arms, they are so cold."

"It cannot be helped, boy; it cannot be helped. Be content. For my long cold arms are not pressing yet on thy heart."

"Do not breathe on me so with thy icy breath. All my strength is departing."

"I must breathe, boy; I must breathe. But do not complain. I am not blowing thee away."

The strange dialogue here came to an end; for to Sintram's surprise he found himself on an open plain, over which the sun was shining brightly, and at no great distance before him he saw his father's castle. While he was thinking whether he might invite the unearthly pilgrim to rest there, this one put an end to his doubts by throwing himself suddenly off the horse, whose wild course was checked by the shock. Raising his forefinger, he said to the boy, "I know old Biorn of the Fiery Eyes well; perhaps but too well. Commend me to him. It will not need to tell him my name; he will recognize me at the description." So saying, the ghastly stranger turned aside into a thick fir-wood, and disappeared rattling amongst the tangled branches.

Slowly and thoughtfully Sintram rode on towards his father's castle, his horse now again quiet and altogether exhausted. He scarcely knew how much he ought to relate of his wonderful journey, and he also felt oppressed with anxiety for the good Rolf, who had remained so far behind. He found himself at the castle-gate sooner than he had expected; the drawbridge was lowered, the doors were thrown open; an attendant led the youth into the great hall, where Biorn was sitting all alone at a huge table, with many flagons and glasses before him, and suits of armour ranged on either side of him. It was his daily custom, by way of company, to have the armour of his ancestors, with closed visors, placed all round the table at which he sat. The father and son began conversing as follows:

"Where is Rolf?"

"I do not know, father; he left me in the mountains."

"I will have Rolf shot if he cannot take better care than that of my only child."

"Then, father, you will have your only child shot at the same time, for without Rolf I cannot live; and if even one single dart is aimed at him, I will be there to receive it, and to shield his true and faithful heart."

"So!—Then Rolf shall not be shot, but he shall be driven from the castle."

"In that case, father, you will see me go away also; and I will give myself up to serve him in forests, in mountains, in caves."

"So!—Well, then, Rolf must remain here."

"That is just what I think, father."

"Were you riding quite alone?"

"No, father; but with a strange pilgrim. He said that he knew you very well —perhaps too well." And thereupon Sintram began to relate and to describe all that had passed with the pale man.

"I know him also very well," said Biorn. "He is half crazed and half wise, as we sometimes are astonished at seeing that people can be. But do thou, my boy, go to rest after thy wild journey. I give you my word that Rolf shall be kindly received if he arrive here; and that if he do not come soon, he shall be sought for in the mountains."

"I trust to your word, father," said Sintram, half humble, half proud; and he did after the command of the grim lord of the castle.

CHAPTER 4

Towards evening Sintram awoke. He saw the good Rolf sitting at his bedside, and looked up in the old man's kind face with a smile of unusually innocent brightness. But soon again his dark brows were knit, and he asked, "How did my father receive you, Rolf? Did he say a harsh word to you?"

"No, my dear young lord, he did not; indeed he did not speak to me at all. At first he looked very wrathful; but he checked himself, and ordered a servant to bring me food and wine to refresh me, and afterwards to take me to your room."

"He might have kept his word better. But he is my father, and I must not judge him too hardly. I will now go down to the evening meal." So saying, he sprang up and threw on his furred mantle.

But Rolf stopped him, and said, entreatingly: "My dear young master, you would do better to take your meal to-day alone here in your own apartment; for there is a guest with your father, in whose company I should be very sorry to see you. If you will remain here, I will entertain you with pleasant tales and songs."

"There is nothing in the world which I should like better, dear Rolf," answered Sintram; "but it does not befit me to shun any man. Tell me, whom should I find with my father?"

"Alas!" said the old man, "you have already found him in the mountain. Formerly, when I used to ride about the country with Biorn, we often met with him, but I was forbidden to tell you anything about him; and this is the first time that he has ever come to the castle."

"The crazy pilgrim!" replied Sintram; and he stood awhile in deep thought, as if considering the matter. At last, rousing himself, he said, "Dear old friend, I would most willingly stay here this evening all alone with you and your stories and songs, and all the pilgrims in the world should not entice me from this quiet room. But one thing must be considered. I feel a kind of dread of that pale, tall man; and by such fears no knight's son can ever suffer himself to be overcome. So be not angry, dear Rolf, if I determine to go and look that strange palmer in the face." And he shut the door of the chamber behind him, and with firm and echoing steps proceeded to the hall.

The pilgrim and the knight were sitting opposite to each other at the great table, on which many lights were burning; and it was fearful, amongst all the lifeless armour, to see those two tall grim men move, and eat, and drink.

As the pilgrim looked up on the boy's entrance, Biorn said: "You know him already: he is my only child, and fellow-traveller this morning."

The palmer fixed an earnest look on Sintram, and answered, shaking his head, "I know not what you mean."

Then the boy burst forth, impatiently, "It must be confessed that you deal very unfairly by us! You say that you know my father but too much, and now it seems that you know me altogether too little. Look me in the face: who allowed you to ride on his horse, and in return had his good steed driven almost wild? Speak, if you can!"

Biorn smiled, shaking his head, but well pleased, as was his wont, with his son's wild behaviour; while the pilgrim shuddered as if terrified and overcome by some fearful irresistible power. At length, with a trembling voice, he said these words: "Yes, yes, my dear young lord, you are surely quite right; you are perfectly right in everything which you may please to assert."

Then the lord of the castle laughed aloud, and said: "Why, thou strange pilgrim, what is become of all thy wonderfully fine speeches and warnings now? Has the boy all at once struck thee dumb and powerless? Beware, thou prophet-messenger, beware!"

But the palmer cast a fearful look on Biorn, which seemed to quench the light of his fiery eyes, and said solemnly, in a thundering voice, "Between me and thee, old man, the case stands quite otherwise. We have nothing to reproach each other with. And now suffer me to sing a song to you on the lute." He stretched out his hand, and took down from the wall a forgotten and half-strung lute, which was hanging there; and, with surprising skill and rapidity, having put it in a state fit for use, he struck some chords, and raised this song to the low melancholy tones of the instrument:

"The flow'ret was mine own, mine own,
But I have lost its fragrance rare,
And knightly name and freedom fair,
Through sin, through sin alone.

The flow'ret was thine own, thine own,

Why cast away what thou didst win?
Thou knight no more, but slave of sin,
Thou'rt fearfully alone!"

"Have a care!" shouted he at the close in a pealing voice, as he pulled the strings so mightily that they all broke with a clanging wail, and a cloud of dust rose from the old lute, which spread round him like a mist.

Sintram had been watching him narrowly whilst he was singing, and more and more did he feel convinced that it was impossible that this man and his fellow-traveller of the morning could be one and the same. Nay, the doubt rose to certainty, when the stranger again looked round at him with the same timid, anxious air, and with many excuses and low reverences hung the lute in its old place, and then ran out of the hall as if bewildered with terror, in strange contrast with the proud and stately bearing which he had shown to Biorn.

The eyes of the boy were now directed to his father, and he saw that he had sunk back senseless in his seat, as if struck by a blow. Sintram's cries called Rolf and other attendants into the hall; and only by great labour did their united efforts awake the lord of the castle. His looks were still wild and disordered; but he allowed himself to be taken to rest, quiet and yielding.

CHAPTER 5

An illness followed this sudden attack; and during the course of it the stout old knight, in the midst of his delirious ravings, did not cease to affirm confidently that he must and should recover. He laughed proudly when his fever-fits came on, and rebuked them for daring to attack him so needlessly. Then he murmured to himself, "That was not the right one yet; there must still be another one out in the cold mountains."

Always at such words Sintram involuntarily shuddered; they seemed to strengthen his notion that he who had ridden with him, and he who had sat at table in the castle, were two quite distinct persons; and he knew not why, but this thought was inexpressibly awful to him. Biorn recovered, and appeared to have entirely forgotten his adventure with the palmer. He hunted in the mountains; he carried on his usual wild warfare with his neighbours; and Sintram, as he grew up, became his almost constant companion; whereby each year a fearful strength of body and spirit was unfolded in the youth. Every one trembled at the sight of his sharp pallid features, his dark rolling eyes, his tall, muscular, and somewhat lean form; and yet no one hated him— not even those whom he distressed or injured in his wildest humours. This might arise in part out of regard to old Rolf, who seldom left him for long,

18

and who always held a softening influence over him; but also many of those who had known the Lady Verena while she still lived in the world affirmed that a faint reflection of her heavenly expression floated over the very unlike features of her son, and that by this their hearts were won.

Once, just at the beginning of spring, Biorn and his son were hunting in the neighbourhood of the sea-coast, over a tract of country which did not belong to them; drawn thither less by the love of sport than by the wish of bidding defiance to a chieftain whom they detested, and thus exciting a feud. At that season of the year, when his winter dreams had just passed off, Sintram was always unusually fierce and disposed for warlike adventures. And this day he was enraged at the chieftain for not coming in arms from his castle to hinder their hunting; and he cursed, in the wildest words, his tame patience and love of peace. Just then one of his wild young companions rushed towards him, shouting joyfully: "Be content my dear young lord! I will wager that all is coming about as we and you wish; for as I was pursuing a wounded deer down to the sea-shore, I saw a sail and a vessel filled with armed men making for the shore. Doubtless your enemy purposes to fall upon you from the coast."

Joyfully and secretly Sintram called all his followers together, being resolved this time to take the combat on himself alone, and then to rejoin his father, and astonish him with the sight of captured foes and other tokens of victory.

The hunters, thoroughly acquainted with every cliff and rock on the coast, hid themselves round the landing-place; and soon the strange vessel hove nearer with swelling sails, till at length it came to anchor, and its crew began to disembark in unsuspicious security. At the head of them appeared a knight of high degree, in blue steel armour richly inlaid with gold. His head was bare, for he carried his costly golden helmet hanging on his left arm. He looked royally around him; and his countenance, which dark brown locks shaded, was pleasant to behold; and a well-trimmed moustache fringed his mouth, from which, as he smiled, gleamed forth two rows of pearl-white teeth.

A feeling came across Sintram that he must already have seen this knight somewhere; and he stood motionless for a few moments. But suddenly he raised his hand, to make the agreed signal of attack. In vain did the good Rolf, who had just succeeded in getting up to him, whisper in his ear that these could not be the foes whom he had taken them for, but that they were unknown, and certainly high and noble strangers.

"Let them be who they may," replied the wild youth, "they have enticed me here to wait, and they shall pay the penalty of thus fooling me. Say not another word, if you value your life." And immediately he gave the signal, a thick shower of javelins followed from all sides, and the Norwegian warriors rushed forth with flashing swords. They found their foes as brave, or somewhat braver, than they could have desired. More fell on the side of those who made than of those who received the assault; and the strangers appeared to understand surprisingly the Norwegian manner of fighting. The knight in steel armour had not in his haste put on his helmet; but it seemed as if he in no wise needed such protection, for his good sword afforded him sufficient defence even against the spears and darts which were incessantly hurled at him, as with rapid skill he received them on the shining blade, and dashed them far away, shivered into fragments.

Sintram could not at the first onset penetrate to where this shining hero was standing, as all his followers, eager after such a noble prey, thronged closely round him; but now the way was cleared enough for him to spring towards the brave stranger, shouting a war-cry, and brandishing his sword above his head.

"Gabrielle!" cried the knight, as he dexterously parried the heavy blow which was descending, and with one powerful sword-thrust he laid the youth prostrate on the ground; then placing his knee on Sintram's breast, he drew forth a flashing dagger, and held it before his eyes as he lay astonished. All at once the men-at-arms stood round like walls. Sintram felt that no hope remained for him. He determined to die as it became a bold warrior; and without giving one sign of emotion, he looked on the fatal weapon with a steady gaze.

As he lay with his eyes cast upwards, he fancied that there appeared suddenly from heaven a wondrously beautiful female form in a bright attire of blue and gold. "Our ancestors told truly of the Valkyrias," murmured he. "Strike, then, thou unknown conqueror."

But with this the knight did not comply, neither was it a Valkyria who had so suddenly appeared, but the beautiful wife of the stranger, who, having advanced to the high edge of the vessel, had thus met the upraised look of Sintram.

"Folko," cried she, in the softest tone, "thou knight without reproach! I know that thou sparest the vanquished."

The knight sprang up, and with courtly grace stretched out his hand to the conquered youth, saying, "Thank the noble lady of Montfaucon for your life and liberty. But if you are so totally devoid of all goodness as to wish to resume the combat, here am I; let it be yours to begin."

Sintram sank, deeply ashamed, on his knees, and wept; for he had often heard speak of the high renown of the French knight Folko of Montfaucon, who was related to his father's house, and of the grace and beauty of his gentle lady Gabrielle.

CHAPTER 6

The Lord of Montfaucon looked with astonishment at his strange foe; and as he gazed on him more and more, recollections arose in his mind of that northern race from whom he was descended, and with whom he had always maintained friendly relations. A golden bear's claw, with which Sintram's cloak was fastened, at length made all clear to him.

"Have you not," said he, "a valiant and far-famed kinsman, called the Sea-king Arinbiorn, who carries on his helmet golden vulture-wings? And is not your father the knight Biorn? For surely the bear's claw on your mantle must be the cognisance of your house."

Sintram assented to all this, in deep and humble shame.

The Knight of Montfaucon raised him from the ground, and said gravely, yet gently, "We are, then, of kin the one to the other; but I could never have believed that any one of our noble house would attack a peaceful man without provocation, and that, too, without giving warning."

"Slay me at once," answered Sintram, "if indeed I am worthy to die by so noble hands. I can no longer endure the light of day."

"Because you have been overcome?" asked Montfaucon. Sintram shook his head.

"Or is it, rather, because you have committed an unknightly action?"

The glow of shame that overspread the youth's countenance said yes to this.

"But you should not on that account wish to die," continued Montfaucon. "You should rather wish to live, that you may prove your repentance, and make your name illustrious by many noble deeds; for you are endowed with a bold spirit and with strength of limb, and also with the eagle-glance of a chieftain. I should have made you a knight this very hour, if you had borne yourself as bravely in a good cause as you have just now in a bad. See to it, that I may do it soon. You may yet become a vessel of high honour."

A joyous sound of shawms and silver rebecks interrupted his discourse. The lady Gabrielle, bright as the morning, had now come down from the ship, surrounded by her maidens; and, instructed in a few words by Folko who was his late foe, she took the combat as some mere trial of arms, saying, "You must not be cast down, noble youth, because my wedded lord has won the prize; for be it known to you, that in the whole world there is but one knight who can boast of not having been overcome by the Baron of Montfaucon. And who can say," continued she, sportively, "whether even that would have happened, had he not set himself to win back the magic ring from me, his lady-love, destined to him, as well by the choice of my own heart as by the will of Heaven!"

Folko, smiling, bent his head over the snow-white hand of his lady; and then bade the youth conduct them to his father's castle.

Rolf took upon himself to see to the disembarking of the horses and valuables of the strangers, filled with joy at the thought that an angel in woman's form had appeared to soften his beloved young master, and perhaps even to free him from that early curse.

Sintram sent messengers in all directions to seek for his father, and to announce to him the arrival of his noble guests. They therefore found the old knight in his castle, with everything prepared for their reception. Gabrielle could not enter the vast dark-looking building without a slight shudder, which was increased when she saw the rolling fiery eyes of its lord; even the pale, dark-haired Sintram seemed to her very fearful; and she sighed to herself, "Oh! what an awful abode have you brought me to visit, my knight! Would that we were once again in my sunny Gascony, or in your knightly Normandy!"

But the grave yet courteous reception, the deep respect paid to her grace and beauty, and to the high fame of Folko, helped to re-assure her; and soon her bird-like pleasure in novelties was awakened through the strange significant appearance of this new world. And besides, it could only be for a passing moment that any womanly fears found a place in her breast when her lord was near at hand, for well did she know what effectual protection that brave Baron was ever ready to afford to all those who were dear to him, or committed to his charge.

Soon afterwards Rolf passed through the great hall in which Biorn and his guests were seated, conducting their attendants, who had charge of the baggage, to their rooms. Gabrielle caught sight of her favourite lute, and desired a page to bring it to her, that she might see if the precious instrument had been injured by the sea-voyage. As she bent over it with earnest attention, and her taper fingers ran up and down the strings, a smile, like the dawn of spring, passed over the dark countenances of Biorn and his son; and both said, with an involuntary sigh, "Ah! if you would but play on that lute, and sing to it! It would be but too beautiful!" The lady looked up at them, well pleased, and smiling her assent, she began this song:—

"Songs and flowers are returning,
And radiant skies of May,
Earth her choicest gifts is yielding,
But one is past away.

The spring that clothes with tend'rest green
Each grove and sunny plain,
Shines not for my forsaken heart,
Brings not my joys again.

Warble not so, thou nightingale,
Upon thy blooming spray,
Thy sweetness now will burst my heart,
I cannot bear thy lay.

For flowers and birds are come again,
And breezes mild of May,
But treasured hopes and golden hours
Are lost to me for aye!"

The two Norwegians sat plunged in melancholy thought; but especially Sintram's eyes began to brighten with a milder expression, his cheeks glowed, every feature softened, till those who looked at him could have fancied they saw a glorified spirit. The good Rolf, who had stood listening to the song, rejoiced thereat from his heart, and devoutly raised his hands in pious gratitude to heaven. But Gabrielle's astonishment suffered her not to take her eyes from Sintram. At last she said to him, "I should much like to know what has so struck you in that little song. It is merely a simple lay of the spring, full of the images which that sweet season never fails to call up in the minds of my countrymen."

"But is your home really so lovely, so wondrously rich in song?" cried the enraptured Sintram. "Then I am no longer surprised at your heavenly beauty, at the power which you exercise over my hard, wayward heart! For a paradise of song must surely send such angelic messengers through the ruder parts of the world." And so saying, he fell on his knees before the lady in an attitude of deep humility. Folko looked on all the while with an approving smile, whilst Gabrielle, in much embarrassment, seemed hardly to know how to treat the half-wild, half-tamed young stranger. After some hesitation, however, she held out her fair hand to him, and said as she gently raised him: "Surely one who listens with such delight to music must himself know how to awaken its strains. Take my lute, and let us hear a graceful inspired song."

But Sintram drew back, and would not take the instrument; and he said, "Heaven forbid that my rough untutored hand should touch those delicate strings! For even were I to begin with some soft strains, yet before long the wild spirit which dwells in me would break out, and there would be an end of the form and sound of the beautiful instrument. No, no; suffer me rather to fetch my own huge harp, strung with bears' sinews set in brass, for in truth I do feel myself inspired to play and sing."

Gabrielle murmured a half-frightened assent; and Sintram having quickly brought his harp, began to strike it loudly, and to sing these words with a voice no less powerful:

"Sir knight, sir knight, oh! whither away
With thy snow-white sail on the foaming spray?"
Sing heigh, sing ho, for that land of flowers!

"Too long have I trod upon ice and snow;
I seek the bowers where roses blow."
Sing heigh, sing ho, for that land of flowers!

He steer'd on his course by night and day
Till he cast his anchor in Naples Bay.
Sing heigh, sing ho, for that land of flowers!

There wander'd a lady upon the strand,
Her fair hair bound with a golden band.
Sing heigh, sing ho, for that land of flowers!

"Hail to thee! hail to thee! lady bright,
Mine own shalt thou be ere morning light."
Sing heigh, sing ho, for that land of flowers!

"Not so, sir knight," the lady replied,
"For you speak to the margrave's chosen bride."
Sing heigh, sing ho, for that land of flowers!

"Your lover may come with his shield and spear,
And the victor shall win thee, lady dear!"
Sing heigh, sing ho, for that land of flowers!

"Nay, seek for another bride, I pray;
Most fair are the maidens of Naples Bay."
Sing heigh, sing ho, for that land of flowers!

"No, lady; for thee my heart doth burn,
And the world cannot now my purpose turn."
Sing heigh, sing ho, for that land of flowers!

Then came the young margrave, bold and brave;
But low was he laid in a grassy grave.
Sing heigh, sing ho, for that land of flowers!

And then the fierce Northman joyously cried,
"Now shall I possess lands, castle, and bride!"
Sing heigh, sing ho, for that land of flowers!

Sintram's song was ended, but his eyes glared wildly, and the vibrations of the harp-strings still resounded in a marvellous manner. Biorn's attitude was again erect; he stroked his long beard and rattled his sword, as if in great delight at what he had just heard. Much shuddered Gabrielle before the wild song and these strange forms, but only till she cast a glance on the Lord of Montfaucon, sat there smiling in all his hero strength, unmoved, the rough uproar passed by him like an autumnal storm.

CHAPTER 7

Some weeks after this, in the twilight of evening, Sintram, very disturbed, came down to the castle-garden. Although the presence of Gabrielle never failed to soothe and calm him, yet if she left the apartment for even a few instants, the fearful wildness of his spirit seemed to return with renewed strength. So even now, after having long and kindly read legends of the olden times to his father Biorn, she had retired to her chamber. The tones of her lute could be distinctly heard in the garden below; but the sounds only drove the bewildered youth more impetuously through the shades of the ancient elms. Stooping suddenly to avoid some overhanging branches, he unexpectedly came upon something against which he had almost struck, and which, at first sight, he took for a small bear standing on its hind legs, with a long and strangely crooked horn on its head. He drew back in surprise and fear. It addressed him in a grating man's voice: "Well, my brave young knight, whence come you? whither go you? wherefore so terrified?" And then first he saw that he had before him a little old man so wrapped up in a rough garment of fur, that scarcely one of his features was visible, and wearing in his cap a strange-looking long feather.

"But whence come YOU and whither go YOU?" returned the angry Sintram. "For of you such questions should be asked. What have you to do in our domains, you hideous little being?"

"Well, well," sneered the other one, "I am thinking that I am quite big enough as I am—one cannot always be a giant. And as to the rest, why should you find fault that I go here hunting for snails? Surely snails do not belong to the game which your high mightinesses consider that you alone have a right to follow! Now, on the other hand, I know how to prepare from them an excellent high-flavoured drink; and I have taken enough for to-day: marvellous fat little beasts, with wise faces like a man's, and long twisted horns on their heads. Would you like to see them? Look here!"

And then he began to unfasten and fumble about his fur garment; but Sintram, filled with disgust and horror, said, "Psha! I detest such animals! Be quiet, and tell me at once who and what you yourself are."

"Are you so bent upon knowing my name?" replied the little man. "Let it content you that I am master of all secret knowledge, and well versed in the most intricate depths of ancient history. Ah! my young sir, if you would only hear them! But you are afraid of me."

"Afraid of you!" cried Sintram, with a wild laugh.

"Many a better man than you has been so before now," muttered the little Master; "but they did not like being told of it any more than you do."

"To prove that you are mistaken," said Sintram, "I will remain here with you till the moon stands high in the heavens. But you must tell me one of your stories the while."

The little man, much pleased, nodded his head; and as they paced together up and down a retired elm-walk, he began discoursing as follows:—

"Many hundred years ago a young knight, called Paris of Troy, lived in that sunny land of the south where are found the sweetest songs, the brightest flowers, and the most beautiful ladies. You know a song that tells of that fair land, do you not, young sir? 'Sing heigh, sing ho, for that land of flowers.'" Sintram bowed his head in assent, and sighed deeply. "Now," resumed the little Master, "it happened that Paris led that kind of life which is not uncommon in those countries, and of which their poets often sing—he would pass whole months together in the garb of a peasant, piping in the woods and mountains and pasturing his flocks. Here one day three beautiful sorceresses appeared to him, disputing about a golden apple; and from him they sought to know which of them was the most beautiful, since to her the golden fruit was to be awarded. The first knew how to give thrones, and sceptres, and crowns; the second could give wisdom and knowledge; and the third could prepare philtres and love-charms which could not fail of securing the affections of the fairest of women. Each one in turn proffered her choicest gifts to the young shepherd, in order that, tempted by them, he might adjudge the apple to her. But as fair women charmed him more than anything else in the world, he said that the third was the most beautiful—her name was Venus. The two others departed in great displeasure; but Venus bid him put on his knightly armour and his helmet adorned with waving feathers, and then she led him to a famous city called Sparta, where ruled the noble Duke Menelaus. His young Duchess Helen was the loveliest woman on earth, and the sorceress offered her to Paris in return for the golden apple. He was most ready to have her and wished for nothing better; but he asked how he was to gain possession of her."

"Paris must have been a sorry knight," interrupted Sintram. "Such things are easily settled. The husband is challenged to a single combat, and he that is victorious carries off the wife."

"But Duke Menelaus was the host of the young knight," said the narrator.

"Listen to me, little Master," cried Sintram; "he might have asked the sorceress for some other beautiful woman, and then have mounted his horse, or weighed anchor, and departed."

"Yes, yes; it is very easy to say so," replied the old man. "But if you only knew how bewitchingly lovely this Duchess Helen was, no room was left for change." And then he began a glowing description of the charms of this wondrously beautiful woman, but likening the image to Gabrielle so closely, feature for feature, that Sintram, tottering, was forced to lean against a tree. The little Master stood opposite to him grinning, and asked, "Well now, could you have advised that poor knight Paris to fly from her?"

"Tell me at once what happened next," stammered Sintram.

"The sorceress acted honourably towards Paris," continued the old man. "She declared to him that if he would carry away the lovely duchess to his own city Troy, he might do so, and thus cause the ruin of his whole house and of his country; but that during ten years he would be able to defend himself in Troy, and rejoice in the sweet love of Helen."

"And he accepted those terms, or he was a fool!" cried the youth.

"To be sure he accepted them," whispered the little Master. "I would have done so in his place! And do you know, young sir, the look of things then was just as they are happening to-day. The newly-risen moon, partly veiled by clouds, was shining dimly through the thick branches of the trees in the silence of evening. Leaning against an old tree, as you now are doing, stood the young enamoured knight Paris, and at his side the enchantress Venus, but so disguised and transformed, that she did not look much more beautiful than I do. And by the silvery light of the moon, the form of the beautiful beloved one was seen sweeping by alone amidst the whispering boughs." He was silent, and like as in the mirror of his deluding words, Gabrielle just then actually herself appeared, musing as she walked alone down the alley of elms.

"Man,—fearful Master,—by what name shall I call you? To what would you drive me?" muttered the trembling Sintram.

"Thou knowest thy father's strong stone castle on the Moon-rocks?" replied the old man. "The castellan and the garrison are true and devoted to thee. It could stand a ten years' siege; and the little gate which leads to the hills is open, as was that of the citadel of Sparta for Paris."

And, in fact, the youth saw through a gate, left open he knew not how, the dim, distant mountains glittering in the moonlight. "And if he did not accept, he was a fool," said the little Master, with a grin, echoing Sintram's former words.

At that moment Gabrielle stood close by him. She was within reach of his grasp, had he made the least movement; and a moonbeam, suddenly breaking forth, transfigured, as it were, her heavenly beauty. The youth had already bent forward—

"My Lord and God, I pray,
Turn from his heart away
This world's turmoil;
And call him to Thy light,
Be it through sorrow's night,
Through pain or toil."

These words were sung by old Rolf at that very time, as he lingered on the still margin of the castle fish-pond, where he prayed alone to Heaven, full of foreboding care. They reached Sintram's ear; he stood as if spellbound and made the Sign of the Cross. Immediately the little master fled away, jumping uncouthly on one leg, through the gates and shutting them after him with a yell.

Gabrielle shuddered, terrified at the wild noise. Sintram approached her softly, and said, offering his arm to her: "Suffer me to lead you back to the castle. The night in these northern regions is often wild and fearful."

CHAPTER 8

They found the two knights drinking wine within. Folko was relating stories in his usual mild and cheerful manner, and Biorn was listening with a moody air, but yet as if, against his will, the dark cloud might pass away before that bright and gentle courtesy. Gabrielle saluted the baron with a smile, and signed to him to continue his discourse, as she took her place near the knight Biorn, full of watchful kindness. Sintram stood by the hearth, abstracted and melancholy; and the embers, as he stirred them, cast a strange glow over his pallid features.

"And of all the German trading-towns," continued Montfaucon, "the largest and richest is Hamburgh. In Normandy we willingly see their merchants land on our coasts, and those excellent people never fail to prove themselves our friends when we seek their advice and assistance. When I first visited Hamburgh, every honour and respect was paid to me. I found its inhabitants engaged in a war with a neighbouring count, and immediately I used my sword for them, vigorously and successfully."

"Your sword! your knightly sword!" interrupted Biorn; and the old wonted fire flashed from his eyes. "Against a knight, and for shopkeepers!"

"Sir knight," replied Folko, calmly, "the barons of Montfaucon have ever used their swords as they chose, without the interference of another; and as I have received this good custom, so do I wish to hand it on. If you agree not to this, so speak it freely out. But I forbid every rude word against the men of Hamburgh, since I have declared them to be my friends."

Biorn cast down his haughty eyes, and their fire faded away. In a low voice he said, "Proceed, noble baron. You are right, and I am wrong."

Then Folko stretched out his hand to him across the table, and resumed his narration: "Amongst all my beloved Hamburghers the dearest to me are two men of marvellous experience—a father and son. What have they not seen and done in the remotest corners of the earth, and instituted in their native town! Praise be to God, my life cannot be called unfruitful; but, compared with the wise Gotthard Lenz and his stout-hearted son Rudlieb, I look upon myself as an esquire who has perhaps been some few times to tourneys, and, besides that, has never hunted out his own forests. They have converted, subdued, gladdened, dark men whom I know not how to name; and the wealth which they have brought back with them has all been devoted to the common weal, as if fit for no other purpose. On their return from their long and perilous sea-voyages, they hasten to an hospital which has been founded by them, and where they undertake the part of overseers, and of careful and patient nurses. Then they proceed to select the most fitting spots whereon to erect new towers and fortresses for the defence of their beloved country. Next they repair to the houses where strangers and travellers receive hospitality at their cost; and at last they return to their own abode, to entertain their guests, rich and noble like kings, and simple and unconstrained like shepherds. Many a tale of their wondrous adventures serves to enliven these sumptuous feasts. Amongst others, I remember to have heard my friends relate one at which my hair stood on end. Possibly I may gain some more complete information on the subject from you. It appears that several years ago, just about the time of the Christmas festival, Gotthard and Rudlieb were shipwrecked on the coast of Norway, during a violent winter tempest. They could never exactly ascertain the situation of the rocks on which their vessel stranded; but so much is certain, that very near the sea-shore stood a huge castle, to which the father and son betook themselves, seeking for that assistance and shelter which Christian people are ever willing to afford each other in case of need. They went alone, leaving their followers to watch the injured ship. The castle- gates were thrown open, and they thought all was well. But on a sudden the court-yard was filled with armed men, who with one accord aimed their sharp iron-pointed spears at the defenceless strangers, whose dignified remonstrances and mild entreaties were only heard in sullen silence or with scornful jeerings. After a while a knight came down the stairs, with fire- flashing eyes. They hardly knew whether to think they saw a spectre, or a wild heathen; he gave a signal, and the fatal spears closed around them. At that instant the soft tones of a woman's voice fell on their ear, calling on the Saviour's holy name for aid; at the sound, the spectres in the court-yard rushed madly one against the other, the gates burst open, and Gotthard and Rudlieb fled away, catching a glimpse as they went of an angelic woman who appeared at one of the windows of the castle. They made every exertion to get their ship again afloat, choosing to trust themselves to the sea rather than to that barbarous coast; and at last, after manifold dangers, they landed at Denmark. They say that some heathen must have owned the cruel castle; but I hold it to be some ruined fortress, deserted by men, in which hellish spectres were wont to hold their nightly meetings. What heathen could be found so demon- like as to offer death to shipwrecked strangers, instead of refreshment and shelter?"

Biorn gazed fixedly on the ground, as though he were turned into stone but Sintram came towards the table, and said, "Father, let us seek out this godless abode, and lay it level with the dust. I cannot tell how, but somehow I feel quite sure that the accursed deed of which we have just heard is alone the cause of my frightful dreams."

Enraged at his son, Biorn rose up, and would perhaps again have uttered some dreadful words; but Heaven decreed otherwise, for just at that moment the pealing notes a trumpet were heard, which drowned the angry tones his voice, the great doors opened slowly, and a herald entered the hall. He bowed reverently, and then said, "I am sent by Jarl Eric the Aged. He returned two days ago from his expedition to the Grecian seas. His wish had been to take vengeance on the island which is called Chios, where fifty years ago his father was slain by the soldiers of the Emperor. But your kinsman, the sea- king Arinbiorn, who was lying there at anchor, tried to pacify him. To this Jarl Eric would not listen; so the sea-king said next that he would never suffer Chios to be laid waste, because it was an island where the lays of an old Greek bard, called Homer, were excellently sung, and where more-over a very choice wine was made. Words proving of no avail, a combat ensued; in which Arinbiorn had so much the advantage that Jarl Eric lost two of his ships, and only with difficulty escaped in one which had already sustained great damage. Eric the Aged has now resolved to take revenge on some of the sea-king's race, since Arinbiorn himself is seldom on the spot. Will you, Biorn of the Fiery Eyes, at once pay as large a penalty in cattle, and money, and goods, as it may please the Jarl to demand? Or will you prepare to meet him with an armed force at Niflung's Heath seven days hence?"

Biorn bowed his head quietly, and replied in a mild tone, "Seven days hence at Niflung's Heath." He then offered to the herald a golden goblet full of rich wine, and added, "Drink that, and then carry off with thee the cup which thou hast emptied."

"The Baron of Montfaucon likewise sends greeting to thy chieftain, Jarl Eric," interposed Folko; "and engages to be also at Niflung's Heath, as the hereditary friend of the sea-king, and also as the kinsman and guest of Biorn of the Fiery Eyes."

The herald was seen to tremble at the name of Montfaucon; he bowed very low, cast an anxious, reverential look at the baron, and left the hall.

Gabrielle looked on her knight, smiling lovingly and securely, for she well knew his victorious prowess; and she only asked, "Where shall I remain, whilst you go forth to battle, Folko?"

"I had hoped," answered Biorn, "that you would be well contented to stay in this castle, lovely lady; I leave my son to guard you and attend on you."

Gabrielle hesitated an instant; and Sintram, who had resumed his position near the fire, muttered to himself as he fixed his eyes on the bright flames which were flashing up, "Yes, yes, so it will probably happen. I can fancy that Duke Menelaus had just left Sparta on some warlike expedition, when the young knight Paris met the lovely Helen that evening in the garden."

But Gabrielle, shuddering although she knew not why, said quickly, "Without you, Folko? And must I forego the joy of seeing you fight? or the honour of tending you, should you chance to receive a wound?"

Folko bowed, gracefully thanking his lady, and replied, "Come with your knight, since such is your pleasure, and be to him a bright guiding star. It is a good old northern custom that ladies should be present at knightly combats, and no true warrior of the north will fail to respect the place whence beams the light of their eyes. Unless, indeed," continued he with an inquiring look at Biorn, "unless Jarl Eric is not worthy of his forefather?"

"A man of honour," said Biorn confidently.

"Then array yourself, my fairest love," said the delighted Folko; "array yourself and come forth with us to the battle-field to behold and judge our deeds."

"Come forth with us to the battle," echoed Sintram in a sudden transport of joy.

And they all dispersed in calm cheerfulness; Sintram betaking himself again to the wood, while the others retired to rest.

CHAPTER 9

It was a wild dreary tract of country that, which bore the name of Niflung's Heath. According to tradition, the young Niflung, son of Hogni, the last of his race, had there ended darkly a sad and unsuccessful life. Many ancient grave-stones were still standing round about; and in the few oak-trees scattered here and there over the plain, huge eagles had built their nests. The beating of their heavy wings as they fought together, and their wild screams, were heard far off in more thickly-peopled regions; and at the sound children would tremble in their cradles, and old men quake with fear as they slumbered over the blazing hearth.

As the seventh night, the last before the day of combat, was just beginning, two large armies were seen descending from the hills in opposite directions; that which came from the west was commanded by Eric the Aged, that from the east by Biorn of the Fiery Eyes. They appeared thus early in compliance with the custom which required that adversaries should always present themselves at the appointed field of battle before the time named, in order to prove that they rather sought than dreaded the fight. Folko forthwith pitched on the most convenient spot the tent of blue samite fringed with gold, which he carried with him to shelter his gentle lady; whilst Sintram, in the character of herald, rode over to Jarl Eric to announce to him that the beauteous Gabrielle of Montfaucon was present in the army of the knight Biorn, and would the next morning be present as a judge of the combat.

Jarl Eric bowed low on receiving this pleasing message; and ordered his bards to strike up a lay, the words of which ran as follows:—

"Warriors bold of Eric's band,
Gird your glittering armour on,
Stand beneath to-morrow's sun,
In your might.

Fairest dame that ever gladden'd
Our wild shores with beauty's vision,

May thy bright eyes o'er our combat,
Judge the right!

Tidings of yon noble stranger
Long ago have reach'd our ears,
Wafted upon southern breezes,
O'er the wave.

Now midst yonder hostile ranks,
In his warlike pride he meets us,
Folko comes! Fight, men of Eric,
True and brave!"

These wondrous tones floated over the plain, and reached the tent of Gabrielle. It was no new thing to her to hear her knight's fame celebrated on all sides; but now that she listened to his praises bursting forth in the stillness of night from the mouth of his enemies, she could scarce refrain from kneeling at the feet of the mighty chieftain. But he with courteous tenderness held her up, and pressing his lips fervently on her soft hand, he said, "My deeds, O lovely lady, belong to thee, and not to me!"

Now the night had passed away, and the east was glowing; and on Niflung's Heath there was waving, and resounding, and glowing too. Knights put on their rattling armour, war-horses began to neigh, the morning draught went round in gold and silver goblets, while war- songs and the clang of harps resounded in the midst. A joyous march was heard in Biorn's camp, as Montfaucon, with his troops and retainers, clad in bright steel armour, conducted their lady up to a neighbouring hill, where she would be safe from the spears which would soon be flying in all directions, and whence she could look freely over the battle-field. The morning sun, as it were in homage, played over her beauty; and as she came in view of the camp of Jarl Eric, his soldiers lowered their weapons, whilst the chieftains bent low the crests of their huge helmets. Two of Montfaucon's pages remained in attendance on Gabrielle; for so noble a service not unwillingly bridling their love of fighting. Both armies passed in front of her, saluting her and singing as they went; they then placed themselves in array, and the fight began.

The spears flew from the hands of the stout northern warriors, rattling against the broad shields under which they sheltered themselves, or sometimes clattering as they met in the air; at intervals, on one side or the other, a man was struck, and fell silent in his blood. Then the Knight of Montfaucon advanced with his troop of Norman horsemen—even as he dashed past, he did not fail to lower his shining sword to salute Gabrielle; and then with an exulting war-cry, which burst from many a voice, they charged the left wing of the enemy. Eric's foot-soldiers, kneeling firmly, received them

with fixed javelins—many a noble horse fell wounded to death, and in falling brought his rider with him to the ground; others again crushed their foes under them in their death-fall. Folko rushed through—he and his war-steed unwounded—followed by a troop of chosen knights. Already were they falling into disorder— already were Biorn's warriors giving shouts of victory
—when a troop of horse, headed by Jarl Eric himself, advanced against the valiant baron; and whilst his Normans, hastily assembled, assisted him in repelling this new attack, the enemy's infantry were gradually forming themselves into a thick mass, which rolled on and on. All these movements seemed caused by a warrior whose loud piercing shout was in the midst. And scarcely were the troops formed into this strange array, when suddenly they spread themselves out on all sides, carrying everything before them with the irresistible force of the burning torrent from Hecla.

Biorn's soldiers, who had thought to enclose their enemies, lost courage and gave way before this wondrous onset. The knight himself in vain attempted to stem the tide of fugitives, and with difficulty escaped being carried away by it.

Sintram stood looking on this scene of confusion with mute indignation; friends and foes passed by him, all equally avoiding him, and dreading to come in contact with one whose aspect was so fearful, nay, almost unearthly, in his motionless rage. He aimed no blow either to right or left; his powerful battle-axe rested in his hand; but his eyes flashed fire, and seemed to be piercing the enemy's ranks through and through, as if he would find out who it was that had conjured up this sudden warlike spirit. He succeeded. A small man clothed in strange-looking armour, with large golden horns on his helmet, and a long visor advancing in front of it, was leaning on a two-edged curved spear, and seemed to be looking with derision at the flight of Biorn's troops as they were pursued by their victorious foes. "That is he," cried Sintram; "he who will drive us from the field before the eyes of Gabrielle!" And with the swiftness of an arrow he flew towards him with a wild shout. The combat was fierce, but not of long duration. To the wondrous dexterity of his adversary, Sintram opposed his far superior size; and he dealt so fearful a blow on the horned helmet, that a stream of blood rushed forth, the small man fell as if stunned, and after some frightful convulsive movements, his limbs appeared to stiffen in death.

His fall gave the signal for that of all Eric's army. Even those who had not seen him fall, suddenly lost their courage and eagerness for the battle, and retreated with uncertain steps, or ran in wild affright on the spears of their enemies. At the same time Montfaucon was dispersing Jarl Eric's cavalry, after a desperate conflict—had hurled their chief from the saddle, and taken him prisoner with his own hand. Biorn of the Fiery Eyes stood victorious in the middle of the field of battle. The day was won.

CHAPTER 10

In sight of both armies, with glowing cheeks and looks of modest humility, Sintram was conducted by the brave baron up the hill where Gabrielle stood in all the lustre of her beauty. Both warriors bent the knee before her, and Folko said, solemnly, "Lady, this valiant youth of a noble race has deserved the reward of this day's victory. I pray you let him receive it from your fair hand."

Gabrielle bowed courteously, took off her scarf of blue and gold, and fastened it to a bright sword, which a page brought to her on a cushion of cloth of silver. She then, with a smile, presented the noble gift to Sintram, who was bending forward to receive it, when suddenly Gabrielle drew back, and turning to Folko, said, "Noble baron, should not he on whom I bestow a scarf and sword be first admitted into the order of knighthood?" Light as a feather, Folko sprang up, and bowing low before his lady, gave the youth the accolade with solemn earnestness. Then Gabrielle buckled on his sword, saying, "For the honour of God and the service of virtuous ladies, young knight. I saw you fight, I saw you conquer, and my earnest prayers followed you. Fight and conquer often again, as you have done this day, that the beams of your renown may shine over my far-distant country." And at a sign from Folko, she offered her tender lips for the new knight to kiss. Thrilling all over, and full of a holy joy, Sintram arose in deep silence, and hot tears streamed down his softened countenance, whilst the shout and the trumpets of the assembled troops greeted the youth with stunning applause. Old Rolf stood silently on one side, and as he looked in the mild beaming eyes of his foster- child, he calmly and piously returned thanks:

"The strife at length hath found its end,
Rich blessings now shall heaven send!
The evil foe is slain!"

Biorn and Jarl Eric had the while been talking together eagerly, but not unkindly. The conqueror now led his vanquished enemy up the hill and presented him to the baron and Gabrielle, saying, "Instead of two enemies you now see two sworn allies; and I request you, my beloved guests and kinsfolk, to receive him graciously as one who henceforward belongs to us."

"He was so always," added Eric, smiling; "I sought, indeed, revenge; but I have now had enough of defeats both by sea and land. Yet I thank Heaven that neither in the Grecian seas, to the sea-king, nor in Niflung's Heath, to you, have I yielded ingloriously."

The Lord of Montfaucon assented cordially, and heartily and solemnly was reconciliation made. Then Jarl Eric addressed Gabrielle with so noble a grace, that with a smile of wonder she gazed on the gigantic grey hero, and gave him her beautiful hand to kiss.

Meanwhile Sintram was speaking earnestly to his good Rolf; and at length he was heard to say, "But before all, be sure that you bury that wonderfully brave knight whom my battle-axe smote. Choose out the greenest hill for his resting-place, and the loftiest oak to shade his grave. Also, I wish you to open his visor, and to examine his countenance carefully, that so, though mortally smitten, we may not bury him alive; and moreover, that you may be able to describe to me him to whom I owe the noblest prize of victory."

Rolf bowed readily, and went.

"Our young knight is speaking there of one amongst the slain of whom I should like to hear more," said Folko, turning to Jarl Eric. "Who, dear Jarl, was that wonderful chieftain who led on your troops so skilfully, and who at last fell under Sintram's powerful battle-axe?"

"You ask me more than I know how to answer," replied Jarl Eric. "About three nights ago this stranger made his appearance amongst us. I was sitting with my chieftains and warriors round the hearth, forging our armour, and singing the while. Suddenly, above the din of our hammering and our singing, we heard so loud a noise that it silenced us in a moment, and we sat motionless as if we had been turned into stone. Before long the sound was repeated; and at last we made out that it must be caused by some person blowing a huge horn outside the castle, seeking for admittance. I went down myself to the gate, and as I passed through the court-yard all my dogs were so terrified by the extraordinary noise, as to be howling and crouching in their kennels instead of barking. I chid them, and called to them, but even the fiercest would not follow me. Then, thought I, I must show you the way to set to work; so I grasped my sword firmly, I set my torch on the ground close beside me, and I let the gates fly open without further delay. For I well knew that it would be no easy matter for any one to come in against my will. A loud laugh greeted me, and I heard these words, 'Well, well, what mighty preparations are these before one small man can find the shelter he seeks!' And in truth I did feel myself redden with shame when I saw the small stranger standing opposite to me quite alone. I called to him to come in at once, and offered my hand to him; but he still showed some displeasure, and would not give me his in return. As he went up, however, he became more friendly—he showed me the golden horn on which he sounded that blast, and which he carried screwed on his helmet, as well as another exactly like it. When he was sitting with us in the hall, he behaved in a very strange manner —sometimes he was merry, sometimes cross; by turns courteous and rude in his demeanour, without any one being able to see a motive for such constant changes. I longed to know where he came from; but how could I ask my guest such a question? He told us as much as this, that he was starved with cold in our country, and that his own was much warmer. Also he appeared well acquainted with the city of Constantinople, and related fearful stories of how brothers, uncles, nephews, nay, even fathers and sons, thrust each other from the throne, blinded, cut out tongues, and murdered. At length he said his own name—it sounded harmonious, like a Greek name, but none of us could remember it. Before long he displayed his skill as an armourer. He understood marvellously well how to handle the red-hot iron, and how to form it into more murderous weapons than any I had ever before seen. I would not suffer him to go on making them, for I was resolved to meet you in the field with equal arms, and such as we are all used to in our northern countries. Then he laughed, and said he thought it would be quite possible to be victorious without them, by skilful movements and the like if only I would entrust the command of my infantry to him, I was sure of victory. Then I thought that he who makes arms well must also wield them well—yet I required some proof of his powers. Ye lords, he came off victorious in trials of strength such as you can hardly imagine; and although the fame of young Sintram, as a bold and brave warrior, is spread far and wide, yet I can scarce believe that he could slay such an one as my Greek ally."

He would have continued speaking, but the good Rolf came hastily back with a few followers, the whole party so ghastly pale, that all eyes were involuntarily fixed on them, and looked anxiously to hear what tidings they had brought. Rolf stood still, silent and trembling.

"Take courage, my old friend!" cried Sintram. "Whatever thou mayest have to tell is truth and light from thy faithful mouth."

"My dear master," began the old man, "be not angry, but as to burying that strange warrior whom you slew, it is a thing impossible. Would that we had never opened that wide hideous visor! For so horrible a countenance grinned at us from underneath it, so distorted by death, and with so hellish an expression, that we hardly kept our senses. We could not by any possibility have touched him. I would rather be sent to kill wolves and bears in the desert, and look on whilst fierce birds of prey feast on their carcases."

All present shuddered, and were silent for a time, till Sintram nerved himself to say, "Dear, good old man, why use such wild words as I never till now heard thee utter? But tell me, Jarl Eric, did your ally appear altogether so awful while he was yet alive?"

"Not as far as I know," answered Jarl Eric, looking inquiringly at his companions, who were standing around. They said the same thing; but on farther questioning, it appeared that neither the chieftain, nor the knights, nor the soldiers, could say exactly what the stranger was like.

"We must then find it out for ourselves, and bury the corpse," said Sintram; and he signed to the assembled party to follow him. All did so except the Lord of Montfaucon, whom the whispered entreaty of Gabrielle kept at her side. He lost nothing thereby. For though Niflung's Heath was searched from one end to the other many times, yet the body of the unknown warrior was no longer to be found.

CHAPTER 11

The joyful calm which came over Sintram on this day appeared to be more than a passing gleam. If too, at times, a thought of the knight Paris and Helen would inflame his heart with bolder and wilder wishes, it needed but one look at his scarf and sword, and the stream of his inner life glided again clear as a mirror, and serene within. "What can any man wish for more than has been already bestowed on me?" would he say to himself at such times in still delight. And thus it went on for a long while.

The beautiful northern autumn had already begun to redden the leaves of the oaks and elms round the castle, when one day it chanced that Sintram was sitting in company with Folko and Gabrielle in almost the very same spot in the garden where he had before met that mysterious being whom, without knowing why, he had named the little Master. But on this day how different did everything appear! The sun was sinking slowly over the sea, the mist of an autumnal evening was rising from the fields and meadows around, towards the hill on which stood the huge castle. Gabrielle, placing her lute in Sintram's hands, said to him, "Dear friend, so mild and gentle as you now are, I may well dare to entrust to you my tender little darling. Let me again hear you sing that lay of the land of flowers; for I am sure that it will now sound much sweeter than when you accompanied it with the vibrations of your fearful harp."

The young knight bowed as he prepared to obey the lady's commands. With a grace and softness hitherto unwonted, the tones resounded from his lips, and the wild song appeared to transform itself, and to bloom into a garden of the blessed. Tears stood in Gabrielle's eyes; and Sintram, as he gazed on the pearly brightness, poured forth tones of yet richer sweetness. When the last notes were sounded, Gabrielle's angelic voice was heard to echo them; and as she repeated,

"Sing heigh, sing ho, for that land of flowers,"

Sintram put down the lute, and sighed with a thankful glance towards the stars, now rising in the heavens. Then Gabrielle, turning towards her lord, murmured these words: "Oh, how long have we been far away from our own shining castles and bright gardens! Oh, for that land of the sweetest flowers!"

Sintram could scarce believe that he heard aright, so suddenly did he feel himself as if shut out from paradise. But his last hope vanished before the courteous assurances of Folko that he would endeavour to fulfil his lady's wishes the very next week, and that their ship was lying off the shore ready to put to sea. She thanked him with a kiss imprinted softly on his forehead; and leaning on his arm, she bent her steps, singing and smiling, towards the castle.

Sintram, troubled in mind, as though turned into stone, remained behind forgotten. At length, when night was now in the sky, he started up wildly, ran up and down the garden, as if all his former madness had again taken possession of him; and then rushed out and wandered upon the wild moonlit hills. There he dashed his sword against the trees and bushes, so that on all sides was heard a sound of crashing and falling. The birds of night flew about him screeching in wild alarm; and the deer, startled by the noise, sprang away and took refuge in the thickest coverts.

On a sudden old Rolf appeared, returning home from a visit to the chaplain of Drontheim, to whom he had been relating, with tears of joy, how Sintram was softened by the presence of the angel Gabrielle, yea, almost healed, and how he dared to hope that the evil dreams had yielded. And now the sword, as it whizzed round the furious youth, had well-nigh wounded the good old man. He stopped short, and clasping his hand, he said, with a deep sigh, "Alas, Sintram! my foster-child, darling of my heart, what has come over thee, thus fearfully stirring thee to rage?"

The youth stood awhile as if spell-bound; he looked in his old friend's face with a fixed and melancholy gaze, and his eyes became dim, like expiring watch-fires seen through a thick cloud of mist. At length he sighed forth these words, almost inaudibly: "Good Rolf, good Rolf, depart from me! thy garden of heaven is no home for me; and if sometimes a light breeze blow open its golden gates, so that I can look in and see the flowery meadow-land where the dear angels dwell, then straightway between them and me come the cold north wind and the icy storm, and the sounding doors fly together, and I remain without, lonely, in endless winter."

"Beloved young knight, oh, listen to me—listen to the good angel within you! Do you not bear in your hand that very sword with which the pure lady girded you? does not her scarf wave over your raging breast? Do you not recollect how you used to say, that no man could wish for more than had fallen to you?"

"Yes, Rolf, I have said that," replied Sintram, sinking on the mossy turf, bitterly weeping. Tears also ran over the old man's white beard. Before long the youth stood again erect, his tears ceased to flow, his looks were fearful, cold, and grim; and he said, "You see, Rolf, I have passed blessed peaceful days, and I thought that the powers of evil would never again have dominion over me. So, perchance, it might have been, as day would ever be did the Sun ever stand in the sky. But ask the poor benighted Earth, wherefore she looks so dark! Bid her again smile as she was wont to do! Old man, she cannot smile; and now that the gentle compassionate Moon has disappeared behind the clouds with her only funeral veil, she cannot even weep. And in this hour of darkness all that is wild and mad wakes up. So, stop me not, I tell thee, stop me not! Hurra, behind, behind the pale Moon!" His voice changed to a hoarse murmur at these last words, storm-like. He tore away from the trembling old man, and rushed through the forest. Rolf knelt down and prayed, and wept silently.

CHAPTER 12

Where the sea-beach was wildest, and the cliffs most steep and rugged, and close by the remains of three shattered oaks, haply marking where, in heathen times, human victims had been sacrificed, now stood Sintram, leaning, as if exhausted, on his drawn sword, and gazing intently on the dancing waves. The moon had again shone forth; and as her pale beams fell on his motionless figure through the quivering branches of the trees, he might have been taken for some fearful idol-image. Suddenly some one on the left half raised himself out of the high withered grass, uttered a faint groan, and again lay down. Then between the two companions began this strange talk:

"Thou that movest thyself so strangely in the grass, dost thou belong to the living or to the dead?"

"As one may take it. I am dead to heaven and joy—I live for hell and anguish."

"Methinks that I have heard thee before."

"Oh, yes."

"Art thou a troubled spirit? and was thy life-blood poured out here of old in sacrifice to idols?"

"I am a troubled spirit; but no man ever has, or ever can, shed my blood. I have been cast down—oh, into a frightful abyss!"

"And didst thou break there thy neck?" "I

live,—and shall live longer than thou."

"Almost thou seemest to me the crazy pilgrim with the dead men's bones."

"I am not he, though often we are companions,—ay, walk together right near and friendly. But to you be it said, he thinks me mad. If sometimes I urge him, and say to him, 'Take!' then he hesitates and points upwards towards the stars. And again, if I say, 'Take not!' then, to a certainty, he seizes on it in some awkward manner, and so he spoils my best joys and pleasures. But, in spite of this, we remain in some measure brothers in arms, and, indeed, all but

43

kinsmen."

"Give me hold of thy hand, and let me help thee to get up."

"Ho, ho! my active young sir, that might bring you no good. Yet, in fact, you have already helped to raise me. Give heed awhile."

Wilder and ever wilder were the strugglings on the ground; thick clouds hurried over the moon and the stars, on a long unknown wild journey; and Sintram's thoughts grew no less wild and stormy, while far and near an awful howling could be heard amidst the trees and the grass. At length the mysterious being arose from the ground. As if with a fearful curiosity, the moon, through a rent in the clouds, cast a beam upon Sintram's companion, and made clear to the shuddering youth that the little Master stood, by him.

"Avaunt!" cried he, "I will listen no more to thy evil stories about the knight Paris: they would end by driving me quite mad."

"My stories about Paris are not needed for that!" grinned the little Master. "It is enough that the Helen of thy heart should be journeying towards Montfaucon. Believe me, madness has thee already, head and heart. Or wouldest thou that she should remain? For that, however, thou must be more courteous to me than thou art now."

Therewith he raised his voice towards the sea, as if fiercely rebuking it, so that Sintram could not but shudder and tremble before the dwarf. But he checked himself, and grasping his sword-hilt with both hands, he said, contemptuously: "Thou and Gabrielle! what acquaintance hast thou with Gabrielle?"

"Not much," was the reply. And the little Master might be seen to quake with fear and rage as he continued: "I cannot well bear the name of thy Helen; do not din it in my ears ten times in a breath. But if the tempest should increase? If the waves should swell, and roll on till they form a foaming ring round the whole coast of Norway? The voyage to Montfaucon must in that case be altogether given up, and thy Helen would remain here, at least through the long, long, dark winter."

"If! if!" replied Sintram, with scorn. "Is the sea thy bond-slave? Are the storms thy fellow-workmen?"

"They are rebels, accursed rebels," muttered the little Master in his red beard. "Thou must lend me thy aid, sir knight, if I am to subdue them; but thou hast not the heart for it."

"Boaster, evil boaster!" answered the youth; "what dost thou ask of me?"

"Not much, sir knight; nothing at all for one who has strength and ardour of

44

soul. Thou needest only look at the sea steadily and keenly for one half-hour, without ever ceasing to wish with all thy might that it should foam and rage and swell, and never again rest till winter has laid its icy hold upon your mountains. Then winter is enough to hinder Duke Menelaus from his voyage to Montfaucon. And now give me a lock of your black hair, which is blowing so wildly about your head, like ravens' or vultures' wings."

The youth drew his sharp dagger, madly cut off a lock of his hair, threw it to the strange being, and now gazed, as he desired, powerfully wishing, on the waves of the sea. And softly, quite softly, did the waters stir themselves, as one whispers in troubled dreams who would gladly rest and cannot. Sintram was on the point of giving up, when in the moonbeams a ship appeared, with white-swelling sails, towards the south. Anguish came over him, that Gabrielle would soon thus quickly sail away; he wished again with all his power, and fixed his eyes intently on the watery abyss. "Sintram," a voice might have said to him— "ah, Sintram, art thou indeed the same who so lately wert gazing on the moistened heaven of the eyes of Gabrielle?"

And now the waters heaved more mightily, and the howling tempest swept over the ocean; the breakers, white with foam, became visible in the moonlight. Then the little Master threw the lock of Sintram's hair up towards the clouds, and, as it was blown to and fro by the blast of wind, the storm burst in all its fury, so that sea and sky were covered with one thick cloud, and far off might be heard the cries of distress from many a sinking vessel.

But the crazy pilgrim with the dead men's bones rose up in the midst of the waves, close to the shore, gigantic, tall, fearfully rocking; the boat in which he stood was hidden from sight, so mightily raged the waves round about it.

"Thou must save him, little Master—thou must certainly save him," cried Sintram's voice, angrily entreating, through the roaring of the winds and waves. But the dwarf replied, with a laugh: "Be quite at rest for him; he will be able to save himself. The waves can do him no harm. Seest thou? They are only begging of him, and therefore they jump up so boldly round him; and he gives them bountiful alms— very bountiful, that I can assure thee."

In fact, as it seemed, the pilgrim threw some bones into the sea, and passed scatheless on his way. Sintram felt his blood run cold with horror, and he rushed wildly towards the castle. His companion had either fled or vanished away.

CHAPTER 13

In the castle, Biorn and Gabrielle and Folko of Montfaucon were sitting round the great stone table, from which, since the arrival of his noble guests, those suits of armour had been removed, formerly the established companions of the lord of the castle, and placed all together in a heap in the adjoining room. At this time, while the storm was beating so furiously against doors and windows, it seemed as if the ancient armour were also stirring in the next room, and Gabrielle several times half rose from her seat in great alarm, fixing her eyes on the small iron door, as though she expected to see an armed spectre issue therefrom, bending with his mighty helmet through the low vaulted doorway.

The knight Biorn smiled grimly, and said, as if he had guessed her thoughts: "Oh, he will never again come out thence; I have put an end to that for ever."

His guests stared at him doubtingly; and with a strange air of unconcern, as though the storm had awakened all the fierceness of his soul, he began the following history:

"I was once a happy man myself; I could smile, as you do, and I could rejoice in the morning as you do; that was before the hypocritical chaplain had so bewildered the wise mind of my lovely wife with his canting talk, that she went into a cloister, and left me alone with our wild boy. That was not fair usage from the fair Verena. Well, so it was, that in the first days of her dawning beauty, before I knew her, many knights sought her hand, amongst whom was Sir Weigand the Slender; and towards him the gentle maiden showed herself the most favourably inclined. Her parents were well aware that Weigand's rank and station were little below their own, and that his early fame as a warrior without reproach stood high; so that before long Verena and he were accounted as affianced. It happened one day that they were walking together in the orchard, when a shepherd was driving his flock up the mountain beyond. The maiden saw a little snow-white lamb frolicking gaily, and longed for it. Weigand vaults over the railings, overtakes the shepherd, and offers him two gold bracelets for the lamb. But the shepherd will not part with it, and scarcely listens to the knight, going quietly the while up the mountain-side, with Weigand close upon him. At last Weigand loses patience. He threatens; and the shepherd, sturdy and proud like all of his race in our northern land, threatens in return. Suddenly Weigand's sword resounds upon his head,—the stroke should have fallen flat, but who can control a fiery horse or a drawn sword? The bleeding shepherd, with a cloven skull, falls down the precipice; his frightened flock bleats on the mountain. Only the little lamb runs in its terror to the orchard, pushes itself through the garden-rails, and lies at Verena's feet, as if asking for help, all red with its master's blood. She took it up in her arms, and from that moment never suffered Weigand the Slender to appear again before her face. She continued to cherish the little lamb, and seemed to take pleasure in nothing else in the world, and became pale and turned towards heaven, as the lilies are. She would soon have taken the veil, but just then I came to aid her father in a bloody war, and rescued him from his enemies. The old man represented this to her, and, softly smiling, she gave me her lovely hand. His grief would not suffer the unhappy Weigand to remain in his own country. It drove him forth as a pilgrim to Asia, whence our forefathers came, and there he did wonderful deeds, both of valour and self- abasement. Truly, my heart was strangely weak when I heard him spoken of at that time. After some years he returned, and wished to build a church or monastery on that mountain towards the west, whence the walls of my castle are distinctly seen. It was said that he wished to become a priest there, but it fell out otherwise. For some pirates had sailed from the southern seas, and, hearing of the building of this monastery, their chief thought to find much gold belonging to the lord of the castle and to the master builders, or else, if he surprised and carried them off, to extort from them a mighty ransom. He did not yet know northern courage and northern weapons; but he soon gained that knowledge. Having landed in the creek under the black rocks, he made his way through a by-path up to the building, surrounded it, and thought in himself that the affair was now ended. Ha! then out rushed Weigand and his builders, and fell upon them with swords and hatchets and hammers. The heathens fled away to their ships, with Weigand behind to take vengeance on them. In passing by our castle he caught a sight of Verena on the terrace, and, for the first time during so many years, she bestowed a courteous and kind salutation on the glowing victor. At that moment a dagger, hurled by one of the pirates in the midst of his hasty flight, struck Weigand's uncovered head, and he fell to the ground bleeding and insensible. We completed the rout of the heathens: then I had the wounded knight brought into the castle; and my pale Verena glowed as lilies in the light of the morning sun, and Weigand opened his eyes with a smile when he was brought near her. He refused to be taken into any room but the small one close to this where the armour is now placed; for he said that he felt as if it were a cell like that which he hoped soon to inhabit in his quiet cloister. All was done after his wish: my sweet Verena nursed him, and he appeared at first to be on the straightest road to recovery; but his head continued weak and liable to be confused by the slightest emotion, his walk was rather a falling than a walking, and his cheeks were colourless. We could not let him go. When we were sitting here together in the evening, he used always to come tottering into the hall through the low doorway; and my heart was sad and wrathful too, when the soft eyes of Verena beamed so sweetly on him, and a glow like that of the evening sky hovered over her lily cheeks. But I bore it, and I could have borne it to the end of our lives,—when, alas! Verena went into a cloister!"

His head fell so heavily on his folded hands, that the stone table seemed to groan beneath it, and he remained a long while motionless as a corpse. When he again raised himself up, his eyes glared fearfully as he looked round the hall, and he said to Folko: "Your beloved Hamburghers, Gotthard Lenz, and Rudlieb his son, they have much to answer for! Who bid them come and be shipwrecked so close to my castle?"

Folko cast a piercing look on him, and a fearful inquiry was on the point of escaping his lips, but another look at the trembling Gabrielle made him silent, at least for the present moment, and the knight Biorn continued his narrative.

"Verena was with her nuns, I was left alone, and my despair had driven me throughout the day through forest and brook and mountain. In the twilight I returned to my deserted castle, and scarcely was I in the hall, when the little door creaked, and Weigand, who had slept through all, crept towards me and asked: 'Where can Verena be?' Then I became as mad, and howled to him, 'She is gone mad, and so am I, and you also, and now we are all mad!' Merciful Heaven, the wound on his head burst open, and a dark stream flowed over his face—ah! how different from the redness when Verena met him at the castle-gate; and he rushed forth, raving mad, into the wilderness without, and ever since has wandered all around as a crazy pilgrim."

He was silent, and so were Folko and Gabrielle, all three pale and cold like images of the dead. At length the fearful narrator added in a low voice, and as if he were quite exhausted: "He has visited me since that time, but he will never again come through the little door. Have I not established peace and order in my castle?"

CHAPTER 14

Sintram had not returned home, when those of the castle betook themselves to rest in deep bewilderment. No one thought of him, for every heart was filled with strange forebodings, and with uncertain cares. Even the heroic breast of the Knight of Montfaucon heaved in doubt.

Old Rolf still remained without, weeping in the forest, heedless of the storm which beat on his unprotected head, while he waited for his young master. But he had gone a very different way; and when the morning dawned, he entered the castle from the opposite side.

Gabrielle's slumbers had been sweet during the whole night. It had seemed to her that angels with golden wings had blown away the wild histories of the evening before, and had wafted to her the bright flowers, the sparkling sea, and the green hills of her own home. She smiled, and drew her breath calmly and softly, whilst the magical tempest raged and howled through the forests, and continued to battle with the troubled sea. But in truth when she awoke in the morning, and heard still the rattling of the windows, and saw the clouds, as if dissolved in mist and steam, still hiding the face of the heavens, she could have wept for anxiety and sadness, especially when she heard from her maidens that Folko had already left their apartment clad in full armour as if prepared for a combat. At the same time she heard the sound of the heavy tread of armed men in the echoing halls, and, on inquiring, found that the Knight of Montfaucon had assembled all his retainers to be in readiness to protect their lady.

Wrapped in a cloak of ermine, she stood trembling like a tender flower just sprung up out of the snow, tottering beneath a winter's storm. Then Sir Folko entered the room, in all his shining armour, and peacefully carrying his golden helmet with the long shadowy plumes in his hand. He saluted Gabrielle with cheerful serenity, and at a sign from him, her attendants retired, while the men-at-arms without were heard quietly dispersing.

"Lady," said he, as he took his seat beside her, on a couch to which he led her, already re-assured by his presence: "lady, will you forgive your knight for having left you to endure some moments of anxiety; but honour and stern justice called him. Now all is set in order, quietly and peacefully; dismiss your fears and every thought that has troubled you, as things which are no more."

"But you and Biorn?" asked Gabrielle. "On the word of a knight," replied he, "all is well there." And thereupon he began to talk over indifferent subjects with his usual ease and wit; but Gabrielle, bending towards him, said with deep emotion:

"O Folko, my knight, the flower of my life, my protector and my dearest hope on earth, tell me all, if thou mayst. But if a promise binds thee, it is different. Thou knowest that I am of the race of Portamour, and I would ask nothing from my knight which could cast even a breath of suspicion on his spotless shield."

Folko thought gravely for one instant; then looking at her with a bright smile, he said: "It is not that, Gabrielle; but canst thou bear what I have to disclose? Wilt thou not sink down under it, as a slender fir gives way under a mass of snow?"

She raised herself somewhat proudly, and said: "I have already reminded thee of the name of my father's house. Let me now add, that I am the wedded wife of the Baron of Montfaucon."

"Then so let it be," replied Folko solemnly; "and if that must come forth openly which should ever have remained hidden in the darkness which belongs to such deeds of wickedness, at least let it come forth less fearfully with a sudden flash. Know then, Gabrielle, that the wicked knight who would have slain my friends Gotthard and Rudlieb is none other than our kinsman and host, Biorn of the Fiery Eyes."

Gabrielle shuddered and covered her eyes with her fair hands; but at the end of a moment she looked up with a bewildered air, and said: "I have heard wrong surely, although it is true that yesterday evening such a thought struck me. For did not you say awhile ago that all was settled and at peace between you and Biorn? Between the brave baron and such a man after such a crime?"

"You heard aright," answered Folko, looking with fond delight on the delicate yet high-minded lady. "This morning with the earliest dawn I went to him and challenged him to a mortal combat in the neighbouring valley, if he were the man whose castle had well-nigh become an altar of sacrifice to Gotthard and Rudlieb. He was already completely armed, and merely saying, 'I am he,' he followed me to the forest. But when he stood alone at the place of combat, he flung away his shield down a giddy precipice, then his sword was hurled after it, and next with gigantic strength he tore off his coat of mail, and said, 'Now fall on, thou minister of vengeance; for I am a heavy sinner, and I dare not fight with thee.' How could I then attack him? A strange truce was agreed on between us. He is half as my vassal, and yet I solemnly forgave him in my own name and in that of my friends. He was contrite, and yet no tear was in his eye, no gentle word on his lips. He is only kept under by the power with which I am endued by having right on my side, and it is on that tenure that Biorn is my vassal. I know not, lady, whether you can bear to see us together on these terms; if not, I will ask for hospitality in some other castle; there are none in Norway which would not receive us joyfully and honourably, and this wild autumnal storm may put off our voyage for many a day. Only this I think, that if we depart directly and in such a manner, the heart of this savage man will break."

"Where my noble lord remains, there I also remain joyfully under his protection," replied Gabrielle; and again her heart glowed with rapture at the greatness of her knight.

CHAPTER 15

The noble lady had just unbuckled her knight's armour with her own fair hands,—on the field of battle alone were pages or esquires bidden handle Montfaucon's armour,—and now she was throwing over his shoulders his mantle of blue velvet embroidered with gold, when the door opened gently, and Sintram entered the room, humbly greeting them. Gabrielle received him kindly, as she was wont, but suddenly turning pale, she looked away and said:

"O Sintram, what has happened to you? And how can one single night have so fearfully altered you?"

Sintram stood still, thunderstruck, and feeling as if he himself did not know what had befallen him. Then Folko took him by the hand, led him towards a bright polished shield, and said very earnestly, "Look here at yourself, young knight!"

At the first glance Sintram drew back horrified. He fancied that he saw the little Master before him with that single upright feather sticking out of his cap; but he at length perceived that the mirror was only showing him his own image and none other, and that his own wild dagger had given him this strange and spectre-like aspect, as he could not deny to himself.

"Who has done that to you?" asked Folko, yet more grave and solemn. "And what terror makes your disordered hair stand on end?"

Sintram knew not what to answer. He felt as if a judgment were coming on him, and a shameful degrading from his knightly rank. Suddenly Folko drew him away from the shield, and taking him towards the rattling window, he asked: "Whence comes this tempest?"

Still Sintram kept silence. His limbs began to tremble under him; and Gabrielle, pale and terrified, whispered, "O Folko, my knight, what has happened? Oh, tell me; are we come into an enchanted castle?"

"The land of our northern ancestors," replied Folko with solemnity, "is full of mysterious knowledge. But we may not, for all that, call its people enchanters; still this youth has cause to watch himself narrowly; he whom the evil one has touched by so much as one hair of his head..."

Sintram heard no more; with a deep groan he staggered out of the room. As he left it, he met old Rolf, still almost benumbed by the cold and storms of the night. Now, in his joy at again seeing his young master, he did not remark his altered appearance; but as he accompanied him to his sleeping-room he said, "Witches and spirits of the tempest must have taken up their abode on the sea-shore. I am certain that such wild storms never arise without some devilish arts."

Sintram fell into a fainting-fit, from which Rolf could with difficulty recover him sufficiently to appear in the great hall at the mid-day hour. But before he went down, he caused a shield to be brought, saw himself therein, and cut close round, in grief and horror, the rest of his long black hair, so that he made himself look almost like a monk; and thus he joined the others already assembled round the table. They all looked at him with surprise; but old Biorn rose up and said fiercely, "Are you going to betake yourself to the cloister, as well as the fair lady your mother?"

A commanding look from the Baron of Montfaucon checked any further outbreak; and as if in apology, Biorn added, with a forced smile, "I was only thinking if any accident had befallen him, like Absalom's, and if he had been obliged to save himself from being strangled by parting with all his hair."

"You should not jest with holy things," answered the baron severely, and all were silent. No sooner was the repast ended, than Folko and Gabrielle, with a grave and courteous salutation, retired to their apartments.

CHAPTER 16

Life in the castle took from this time quite another form. Those two bright beings, Folko and Gabrielle, spent most part of the day in their apartments, and when they showed themselves, it was with quiet dignity and grave silence, while Biorn and Sintram stood before them in humble fear. Nevertheless, Biorn could not bear the thought of his guests seeking shelter in any other knight's abode. When Folko once spoke of it, something like a tear stood in the wild man's eye. His head sank, and he said softly, "As you please; but I feel that if you go, I shall run among the rocks for days."

And thus they all remained together; for the storm continued to rage with such increasing fury over the sea, that no sea voyage could be thought of, and the oldest man in Norway could not call to mind such an autumn. The priests examined all the runic books, the bards looked through their lays and tales, and yet they could find no record of the like. Biorn and Sintram braved the tempest; but during the few hours in which Folko and Gabrielle showed themselves, the father and son were always in the castle, as if respectfully waiting upon them; the rest of the day—nay, often through whole nights, they rushed through the forests and over the rocks in pursuit of bears. Folko the while called up all the brightness of his fancy, all his courtly grace, in order to make Gabrielle forget that she was living in this wild castle, and that the long, hard northern winter was setting in, which would ice them in for many a month. Sometimes he would relate bright tales; then he would play the liveliest airs to induce Gabrielle to lead a dance with her attendants; then, again, handing his lute to one of the women, he would himself take a part the dance, well knowing to express thereby after some new fashion his devotion to his lady. Another time he would have the spacious halls of the castle prepared for his armed retainers to go through their warlike exercises, and Gabrielle always adjudged the reward to the conqueror. Folko often joined the circle of combatants; so that he only met their attacks, defending himself, but depriving no one of the prize. The Norwegians, who stood around as spectators, used to compare him to the demi-god Baldur, one of the heroes of their old traditions, who was wont to let the darts of his companions be all hurled against him, conscious that he was invulnerable, and of his own indwelling strength.

At the close of one of these martial exercises, old Rolf advanced towards Folko, and beckoning him with an humble look, said softly, "They call you the beautiful mighty Baldur,—and they are right. But even the beautiful mighty Baldur did not escape death. Take heed to yourself." Folko looked at him wondering. "Not that I know of any treachery," continued the old man; "or that I can even foresee the likelihood of any. God keep a Norwegian from such a fear. But when you stand before me in all the brightness of your glory, the fleetingness of everything earthly weighs down my mind, and I cannot refrain from saying, 'Take heed, noble baron! oh, take heed! Even the most beautiful glory comes to an end.'"

"Those are wise and pious thoughts," replied Folko calmly, "and I will treasure them in a pure heart."

The good Rolf was often with Folko and Gabrielle, and made a connecting link between the two widely differing parties in the castle. For how could he have ever forsaken his own Sintram! Only in the wild hunting expeditions through the howling storms and tempests he no longer was able to follow his young lord.

At length the icy reign of winter began in all its glory. On this account a return to Normandy was impossible, and therefore the magical storm was lulled. The hills and valleys shone brilliantly in their white attire of snow, and Folko used sometimes, with skates on his feet, to draw his lady in a light sledge over the glittering frozen lakes and streams. On the other hand, the bear-hunts of the lord of the castle and his son took a still more desperate and to them joyous course.

About this time,—when Christmas was drawing near, and Sintram was seeking to overpower his dread of the awful dreams by the most daring expeditions,—about this time, Folko and Gabrielle stood together on one of the terraces of the castle. The evening was mild; the snow- clad fields were glowing in the red light of the setting sun; from below there were heard men's voices singing songs of ancient heroic times, while they worked in the armourer's forge. At last the songs died away, the beating of hammers ceased, and, without the speakers being seen, or there being any possibility of distinguishing them by their voices, the following discourse arose:—

"Who is the bravest amongst all those whose race derives its origin from our renowned land?"

"It is Folko of Montfaucon."

"Rightly said; but tell me, is there anything from which even this bold baron draws back?"

"In truth there is one thing,—and we who have never left Norway face it quite willingly and joyfully."

"And that is—?"

"A bear-hunt in winter, over trackless plains of snow, down frightful ice-covered precipices."

"Truly thou answerest aright, my comrade. He who knows not how to fasten our skates on his feet, how to turn in them to the right or left at a moment's warning, he may be a valiant knight in other respects, but he had better keep away from our hunting parties, and remain with his timid wife in her apartments." At which the speakers were heard to laugh well pleased, and then to betake themselves again to their armourer's work.

Folko stood long buried in thought. A glow beyond that of the evening sky reddened his cheek. Gabrielle also remained silent, considering she knew not what. At last she took courage, and embracing her beloved, she said: "To-morrow thou wilt go forth to hunt the bear, wilt thou not? and thou wilt bring the spoils of the chase to thy lady?"

The knight gave a joyful sign of assent; and the rest of the evening was spent in dances and music.

CHAPTER 17

"See, my noble lord," said Sintram the next morning, when Folko had expressed his wish of going out with him, "these skates of ours give such wings to our course, that we go down the mountain-side swiftly as the wind; and even in going up again we are too quick for any one to be able to pursue us, and on the plains no horse can keep up with us; and yet they can only be worn with safety by those who are well practised. It seems as though some strange spirit dwelt in them, which is fearfully dangerous to any that have not learnt the management of them in their childhood."

Folko answered somewhat proudly: "Do you suppose that this is the first time that I have been amongst your mountains? Years ago I have joined in this sport, and, thank Heaven, there is no knightly exercise which does not speedily become familiar to me."

Sintram did not venture to make any further objections, and still less did old Biorn. They both felt relieved when they saw with what skill and ease Folko buckled the skates on his feet, without suffering any one to assist him. This day they hunted up the mountain in pursuit of a fierce bear which had often before escaped from them. Before long it was necessary that they should separate, and Sintram offered himself as companion to Folko, who, touched by the humble manner of the youth, and his devotion to him, forgot all that had latterly seemed mysterious in the pale altered being before him, and agreed heartily. As now they continued to climb higher and higher up the mountain, and saw from many a giddy height the rocks and crags below them looking like a vast expanse of sea suddenly turned into ice whilst tossed by a violent tempest, the noble Montfaucon drew his breath more freely. He poured forth war-songs and love-longs in the clear mountain air, and the startled echoes repeated from rock to rock the lays of his Frankish home. He sprang lightly from one precipice to another, using strongly and safely his staff for support, and turning now to the right, now to the left, as the fancy seized him; so that Sintram was fain to exchange his former anxiety for a wondering admiration, and the hunters, whose eyes had never been taken off the baron, burst forth with loud applause, proclaiming far and wide fresh glory of their guest.

The good fortune which usually accompanied Folko's deeds of arms seemed still unwilling to leave him. After a short search, he and Sintram found distinct traces of the savage animal, and with beating hearts they followed the track so swiftly that even a winged enemy would have been unable to escape from them. But the creature whom they sought did not attempt a flight—he lay sulkily in a cavern near the top of a steep precipitous rock, infuriated by the shouts of the hunters, and only waiting in his lazy fury for some one to be bold enough to climb up to his retreat, that he might tear him to pieces. Folko and Sintram had now reached the foot of this rock, the rest of the hunters being dispersed over the far-extending plain. The track led the two companions up the rock, and they set about climbing on the opposite sides of it, that they might be the more sure of not missing their prey. Folko reached the lonely topmost point first, and cast his eyes around. A wide, boundless tract of country, covered with untrodden snow, was spread before him, melting in the distance into the lowering clouds of the gloomy evening sky. He almost thought that he must have missed the traces of the fearful beast; when close beside him from a cleft in the rock issued a long growl, and a huge black bear appeared on the snow, standing on its hind legs, and with glaring eyes it advanced towards the baron. Sintram the while was struggling in vain to make his way up the rock against the masses of snow continually slipping down.

Joyful at a combat so long untried as almost to be new, Folko of Montfaucon levelled his hunting spear, and awaited the attack of the wild beast. He suffered it to approach so near that its fearful claws were almost upon him; then he made a thrust, and the spear-head was buried deep in the bear's breast. But the furious beast still pressed on with a fierce growl, kept up on its hind legs by the cross-iron of the spear, and the knight was forced to plant his feet deep in the earth to resist the savage assault; and ever close before him the grim and bloody face of the bear, and close in his ear its deep savage growl, wrung forth partly by the agony of death, partly by thirst for blood. At length the bear's resistance grew weaker, and the dark blood streamed freely upon the snow; he tottered; and one powerful thrust hurled him backwards over the edge of the precipice. At the same instant Sintram stood by the Baron of Montfaucon. Folko said, drawing a deep breath: "But I have not yet the prize in my hands, and have it I must, since fortune has given me a claim to it. Look, one of my skates seems to be out of order. Thinkest thou, Sintram, that it holds enough to slide down to the foot of the precipice?"

"Let me go instead," said Sintram. "I will bring you the head and the claws of the bear."

"A true knight," replied Folko, with some displeasure, "never does a knightly deed by halves. What I ask is, whether my skate will still hold?"

As Sintram bent down to look, and was on the point of saying "No!" he suddenly heard a voice close to him, saying, "Why, yes, to be sure; there is no doubt about it."

Folko thought that Sintram had spoken, and slid down with the swiftness of an arrow, whilst his companion looked up in great surprise. The hated form of the little Master met his eyes. As he was going to address him with angry words, he heard the sound of the baron's fearful fall, and he stood still in silent horror. There was a breathless silence also in the abyss below.

"Now, why dost thou delay?" said the little Master, after a pause. "He is dashed to pieces. Go back to the castle, and take the fair Helen to thyself."

Sintram shuddered. Then his hateful companion began to praise Gabrielle's charms in so glowing, deceiving words, that the heart of the youth swelled with emotions he had never before known. He only thought of him who was now lying at the foot of the rock as of an obstacle removed between him and heaven: he turned towards the castle.

But a cry was heard below: "Help! help! my comrade! I am yet alive, but I am sorely wounded."

Sintram's will was changed, and he called to the baron, "I am coming."

But the little Master said, "Nothing can be done to help Duke Menelaus; and the fair Helen knows it already. She is only waiting for knight Paris to comfort her." And with detestable craft he wove in that tale with what was actually happening, bringing in the most highly wrought praises of the lovely Gabrielle; and alas! the dazzled youth yielded to him, and fled! Again he heard far off the baron's voice calling to him, "Knight Sintram, knight Sintram, thou on whom I bestowed the holy order, haste to me and help me! The she-bear and her whelps will be upon me, and I cannot use my right arm! Knight Sintram, knight Sintram, haste to help me!"

His cries were overpowered by the furious speed with which the two were carried along on their skates, and by the evil words of the little Master, who was mocking at the late proud bearing of Duke Menelaus towards the poor Sintram. At last he shouted, "Good luck to you, she-bear! good luck to your whelps! There is a glorious meal for you! Now you will feed upon the fear of Heathendom, him at whose name the Moorish brides weep, the mighty Baron of Montfaucon. Never again, O dainty knight, will you shout at the head of your troops, 'Mountjoy St. Denys!'" But scarce had this holy name passed the lips of the little Master, than he set up a howl of anguish, writhing himself

58

with horrible contortions, and wringing his hands, and ended by disappearing in a storm of snow which then arose.

Sintram planted his staff firmly in the ground, and stopped. How strangely did the wide expanse of snow, the distant mountains rising above it, and the dark green fir-woods—how strangely did they all look at him in cold reproachful silence! He felt as if he must sink under the weight of his sorrow and his guilt. The bell of a distant hermitage came floating sadly over the plain. With a burst of tears he exclaimed, as the darkness grew thicker round him, "My mother! my mother! I had once a beloved tender mother, and she said I was a good child!" A ray of comfort came to him as if brought on an angel's wing; perhaps Montfaucon was not yet dead! and he flew like lightning along the path, back to the steep rock. When he got to the fearful place, he stooped and looked anxiously down the precipice. The moon, just risen in full majesty, helped him. The Knight of Montfaucon, pale and bleeding, was half kneeling against the rock; his right arm, crushed in his fall, hung powerless at his side; it was plain that he could not draw his good sword out of the scabbard. But nevertheless he was keeping the bear and her young ones at bay by his bold threatening looks, so that they only crept round him, growling angrily; every moment ready for a fierce attack, but as often driven back affrighted at the majestic air by which he conquered even when defenceless.

"Oh! what a hero would there have perished!" groaned Sintram, "and through whose guilt?" In an instant his spear flew with so true an aim that the bear fell weltering in her blood; the young ones ran away howling.

The baron looked up with surprise. His countenance beamed as the light of the moon fell upon it, grave and stern, yet mild, like some angelic vision. "Come down!" he beckoned; and Sintram slid down the side of the precipice, full of anxious haste. He was going to attend to the wounded man, but Folko said, "First cut off the head and claws of the bear which I slew. I promised to bring the spoils of the chase to my lovely Gabrielle. Then come to me, and bind up my wounds. My right arm is broken." Sintram obeyed the baron's commands. When the tokens of victory had been secured, and the broken arm bound up, Folko desired the youth to help him back to the castle.

"O Heavens!" said Sintram in a low voice, "if I dared to look in your face! or only knew how to come near you!"

"Thou wert indeed going on in an evil course," said Montfaucon, gravely; "but how could we, any of us, stand before God, did not repentance help us? At any rate, thou hast now saved my life, and let that thought cheer thy heart."

The youth with tenderness and strength supported the baron's left arm, and they both went their way silently in the moonlight.

CHAPTER 18

Sounds of wailing were heard from the castle as they approached; the chapel was solemnly lighted up; within it knelt Gabrielle, lamenting for the death of the Knight of Montfaucon.

But how quickly was all changed, when the noble baron, pale indeed, and bleeding, yet having escaped all mortal danger, stood smiling at the entrance of the holy building, and said, in a low, gentle voice, "Look up, Gabrielle, and be not affrighted; for, by the honour of my race, thy knight still lives." Oh! with what joy did Gabrielle's eyes sparkle, as she turned to her knight, and then raised them again to heaven, still streaming, but from the deep source of thankful joy! With the help of two pages, Folko knelt down beside her, and they both sanctified their happiness with a silent prayer.

When they left the chapel, the wounded knight being tenderly supported by his lady, Sintram was standing without in the darkness, himself as gloomy as the night, and, like a bird of the night, shunning the sight of men. Yet he came trembling forward into the torch-light, laid the bear's head and claws at the feet of Gabrielle, and said, "The noble Folko of Montfaucon presents the spoils of to- day's chase to his lady."

The Norwegians burst forth with shouts of joyful surprise at the stranger knight, who in the very first hunting expedition had slain the most fearful and dangerous beast of their mountains.

Then Folko looked around with a smile as he said, "And now none of you must jeer at me, if I stay at home for a short time with my timid wife."

Those who the day before had talked together in the armourer's forge came out from the crowd, and bowing low, they replied, "Noble baron, who could have thought that there was no knightly exercise in the whole world in the which you would not show yourself far above all other men?"

"The pupil of old Sir Hugh may be somewhat trusted," answered Folko kindly. "But now, you bold northern warriors, bestow some praises also on my deliverer, who saved me from the claws of the she-bear, when I was leaning against the rock wounded by my fall."

He pointed to Sintram, and the general shout was again raised; and old Rolf, with tears of joy in his eyes, bent his head over his foster-son's hand. But Sintram drew back shuddering.

"Did you but know," said he, "whom you see before you, all your spears would be aimed at my heart; and perhaps that would be the best thing for me. But I spare the honour of my father and of his race, and for this time I will not confess. Only this much must you know, noble warriors—"

"Young man," interrupted Folko with a reproving look, "already again so wild and fierce? I desire that thou wilt hold thy peace about thy dreaming fancies."

Sintram was silenced for a moment; but hardly had Folko begun smilingly to move towards the steps of the castle, than he cried out, "Oh, no, no, noble wounded knight, stay yet awhile; I will serve thee in everything that thy heart can desire; but herein I cannot serve thee. Brave warriors, you must and shall know so much as this; I am no longer worthy to live under the same roof with the noble Baron of Montfaucon and his angelic wife Gabrielle. And you, my aged father, good-night; long not for me. I intend to live in the stone fortress on the Rocks of the Moon, till a change of some kind come over me."

There was that in his way of speaking against which no one dared to set himself, not even Folko.

The wild Biorn bowed his head humbly, and said, "Do according to thy pleasure, my poor son; for I fear that thou art right."

Then Sintram walked solemnly and silently through the castle-gate, followed by the good Rolf. Gabrielle led her exhausted lord up to their apartments.

CHAPTER 19

That was a mournful journey on which the youth and his aged foster-father went towards the Rocks of the Moon, through the wild tangled paths of the snow-clad valleys. Rolf from time to time sang some verses of hymns, in which comfort and peace were promised to the penitent sinner, and Sintram thanked him for them with looks of grateful sadness. Neither of them spoke a word else.

At length, when the dawn of day was approaching, Sintram broke silence by saying, "Who are those two sitting yonder by the frozen stream—a tall man and a little one? Their own wild hearts must have driven them also forth into the wilderness. Rolf, dost thou know them? The sight of them makes me shudder."

"Sir," answered the old man, "your disturbed mind deceives you. There stands a lofty fir-tree, and the old weather-beaten stump of an oak, half-covered with snow, which gives them a somewhat strange appearance. There are no men sitting yonder."

"But, Rolf, look there! look again carefully! Now they move, they whisper together."

"Sir, the morning breeze moves the branches, and whistles in the sharp pine-leaves and in the yellow oak-leaves, and rustles the crisp snow."

"Rolf, now they are both coming towards us. Now they are standing before us, quite close."

"Sir, it is we who get nearer to them as we walk on, and the setting moon throws such long giant-like shadows over the plain."

"Good-evening!" said a hollow voice; and Sintram knew it was the crazy pilgrim, near to whom stood the malignant little Master, looking more hideous than ever.

"You are right, sir knight," whispered Rolf, as he drew back behind Sintram, and made the Sign of the Cross on his breast and his forehead.

The bewildered youth, however, advanced towards the two figures, and said, "You have always taken wonderful pleasure in being my companions. What do you expect will come of it? And do you choose to go now with me to the stone fortress? There I will tend thee, poor pale pilgrim; and as to thee, frightful Master, most evil dwarf, I will make thee shorter by the head, to reward thee for thy deeds yesterday."

"That would be a fine thing," sneered the little Master; "and perhaps thou imaginest that thou wouldst be doing a great service to the whole world? And, indeed, who knows? Something might be gained by it! Only, poor wretch, thou canst not do it."

The pilgrim meantime was waving his pale head to and fro thoughtfully, saying, "I believe truly that thou wouldst willingly have me, and I would go to thee willingly, but I may not yet. Have patience awhile; thou wilt yet surely see me come, but at a distant time; and first we must again visit thy father together, and then also thou wilt learn to call me by my right name, my poor friend."

"Beware of disappointing me again!" said the little Master to the pilgrim in a threatening voice; but he, pointing with his long, shrivelled hand towards the sun, which was just now rising, said, "Stop either that sun or me, if thou canst!"

Then the first rays fell on the snow, and the little Master ran, muttering, down a precipice; but the pilgrim walked on in the bright beams, calmly and with great solemnity, towards a neighbouring castle on the mountain. It was not long before its chapel-bell was heard tolling for the dead.

"For Heaven's sake," whispered the good Rolf to his knight—"for Heaven's sake, Sir Sintram, what kind of companions have you here? One of them cannot bear the light of God's blessed sun, and the other has no sooner set foot in a dwelling than tidings of death wail after his track. Could he have been a murderer?"

"I do not think that," said Sintram. "He seemed to me the best of the two. But it is a strange wilfulness of his not to come with me. Did I not invite him kindly? I believe that he can sing well, and he should have sung to me some gentle lullaby. Since my mother has lived in a cloister, no one sings lullabies to me any more."

At this tender recollection his eyes were bedewed with tears. But he did not himself know what he had said besides, for there was wildness and confusion in his spirit. They arrived at the Rocks of the Moon, and mounted up to the stone fortress. The castellan, an old, gloomy man, the more devoted to the young knight from his dark melancholy and wild deeds, hastened to lower the drawbridge. Greetings were exchanged in silence, and in silence did Sintram enter, and those joyless gates closed with a crash behind the future recluse.

CHAPTER 20

Yes truly, a recluse, or at least something like it, did poor Sintram now become! For towards the time of the approaching Christmas festival his fearful dreams came over him, and seized him so fiercely, that all the esquires and servants fled with shrieks out of the castle, and would never venture back again. No one remained with him except Rolf and the old castellan. After a while, indeed, Sintram became calm, but he went about looking so pallid and still that he might have been taken for a wandering corpse. No comforting of the good Rolf, no devout soothing lays, were of any avail; and the castellan, with his fierce, scarred features, his head almost entirely bald from a huge sword-cut, his stubborn silence, seemed like a yet darker shadow of the miserable knight. Rolf often thought of going to summon the holy chaplain of Drontheim; but how could he have left his lord alone with the gloomy castellan, a man who at all times raised in him a secret horror? Biorn had long had this wild strange warrior in his service, and honoured him on account of his unshaken fidelity and his fearless courage, though neither the knight nor any one else knew whence the castellan came, nor, indeed, exactly who he was. Very few people knew by what name to call him; but that was the more needless, since he never entered into discourse with any one. He was the castellan of the stone fortress on the Rocks of the Moon, and nothing more.

Rolf committed his deep heartfelt cares to the merciful God, trusting that he would soon come to his aid; and the merciful God did not fail him. For on Christmas eve the bell at the drawbridge sounded, and Rolf, looking over the battlements, saw the chaplain of Drontheim standing there, with a companion indeed that surprised him,—for close beside him appeared the crazy pilgrim, and the dead men's bones on his dark mantle shone very strangely in the glimmering starlight: but the sight of the chaplain filled the good Rolf too full of joy to leave room for any doubt in his mind; for, thought he, whoever comes with him cannot but be welcome! And so he let them both in with respectful haste, and ushered them up to the hall, where Sintram, pale and with a fixed look, was sitting under the light of one flickering lamp. Rolf was obliged to support and assist the crazy pilgrim up the stairs, for he was quite benumbed with cold.

"I bring you a greeting from your mother," said the chaplain as he came in; and immediately a sweet smile passed over the young knight's countenance, and its deadly pallidness gave place to a bright soft glow.

"O Heaven!" murmured he, "does then my mother yet live, and does she care to know anything about me?"

"She is endowed with a wonderful presentiment of the future," replied the chaplain; "and all that you ought either to do or to leave undone is faithfully mirrored in various ways in her mind, during a half- waking trance. Now she knows of your deep sorrow, and she sends me, the father-confessor of her convent, to comfort you, but at the same time to warn you; for, as she affirms, and as I am also inclined to think, many strange and heavy trials lie before you."

Sintram bowed himself towards the chaplain with his arms crossed over his breast, and said, with a gentle smile, "Much have I been favoured—more, a thousand times more, than I could have dared to hope in my best hours—by this greeting from my mother, and your visit, reverend sir; and all after falling more fearfully low than I had ever fallen before. The mercy of the Lord is great; and how heavy soever may be the weight and punishment which He may send, I trust, with His grace, to be able to bear it."

Just then the door opened, and the castellan came in with a torch in his hand, the red glare of which made his face look the colour of blood. He cast a terrified glance at the crazy pilgrim, who had just sunk back in a swoon, and was supported on his seat and tended by Rolf; then he stared with astonishment at the chaplain, and at last murmured, "A strange meeting! I believe that the hour for confession and reconciliation is now arrived."

"I believe so too," replied the priest, who had heard his low whisper; "this seems to be truly a day rich in grace and peace. That poor man yonder, whom I found half-frozen by the way, would make a full confession to me at once, before he followed me to a place of shelter. Do as he has done, my dark-browed warrior, and delay not your good purpose for one instant."

Thereupon he left the room with the willing castellan, but he turned back to say, "Sir Knight and your esquire! take good care the while of my sick charge."

Sintram and Rolf did according to the chaplain's desire: and when at length their cordials made the pilgrim open his eyes once again, the young knight said to him, with a friendly smile, "Seest thou? thou art come to visit me after all. Why didst thou refuse me when, a few nights ago, I asked thee so earnestly to come? Perhaps I may have spoken wildly and hastily. Did that scare thee away?"

A sudden expression of fear came over the pilgrim's countenance; but soon he again looked up at Sintram with an air of gentle humility, saying, "O my dear, dear lord, I am most entirely devoted to you— only never speak to me of former passages between you and me. I am terrified whenever you do it. For, my lord, either I am mad and have forgotten all that is past, or that Being has met you in the wood, whom I look upon as my very powerful twin brother."

Sintram laid his hand gently on the pilgrim's mouth, as he answered, "Say nothing more about that matter: I most willingly promise to be silent."

Neither he nor old Rolf could understand what appeared to them so awful in the whole matter; but both shuddered.

After a short pause the pilgrim said, "I would rather sing you a song—a soft, comforting song. Have you not a lute here?"

Rolf fetched one; and the pilgrim, half-raising himself on the couch, sang the following words:

"When death is coming near,
When thy heart shrinks in fear
And thy limbs fail,
Then raise thy hands and pray
To Him who smooths thy way
Through the dark vale.

Seest thou the eastern dawn,
Hearst thou in the red morn
The angel's song?
Oh, lift thy drooping head,
Thou who in gloom and dread
Hast lain so long.

Death comes to set thee free;
Oh, meet him cheerily
As thy true friend,
And all thy fears shall cease,
And in eternal peace
Thy penance end."

"Amen," said Sintram and Rolf, folding their hands; and whilst the last chords of the lute still resounded, the chaplain and the castellan came slowly and gently into the room. "I bring a precious Christmas gift," said the priest. "After many sad years, hope of reconciliation and peace of conscience are returning to a noble, disturbed mind. This concerns thee, beloved pilgrim; and do thou, my Sintram, with a joyful trust in God, take encouragement and example from it."

"More than twenty years ago," began the castellan, at a sign from the chaplain—"more than twenty years ago I was a bold shepherd, driving my flock up the mountains. A young knight followed me, whom they called Weigand the Slender. He wanted to buy of me my favourite little lamb for his fair bride, and offered me much red gold for it. I sturdily refused. Over-bold youth boiled up in us both. A stroke of his sword hurled me senseless down the precipice.

"Not killed?" asked the pilgrim in a scarce audible voice.

"I am no ghost," replied the castellan, somewhat morosely; and then, after an earnest look from the priest, he continued, more humbly: "I recovered slowly and in solitude, with the help of remedies which were easily found by me, a shepherd, in our productive valleys. When I came back into the world, no man knew me, with my scarred face, and my now bald head. I heard a report going through the country, that on account of this deed of his, Sir Weigand the Slender had been rejected by his fair betrothed Verena, and how he had pined away, and she had wished to retire into a convent, but her father had persuaded her to marry the great knight Biorn. Then there came a fearful thirst for vengeance into my heart, and I disowned my name, and my kindred, and my home, and entered the service of the mighty Biorn, as a strange wild man, in order that Weigand the Slender should always remain a murderer, and that I might feed on his anguish. So have I fed upon it for all these long years; I have fed frightfully upon his self-imposed banishment, upon his cheerless return home, upon his madness. But to-day—" and hot tears gushed from his eyes— "but to- day God has broken the hardness of my heart; and, dear Sir Weigand, look upon yourself no more as a murderer, and say that you will forgive me, and pray for him who has done you so fearful an injury, and—"

Sobs choked his words. He fell at the feet of the pilgrim, who with tears of joy pressed him to his heart, in token of forgiveness.

CHAPTER 21

The joy of this hour passed from its first overpowering brightness to the calm, thoughtful aspect of daily life; and Weigand, now restored to health, laid aside the mantle with dead men's bones, saying: "I had chosen for my penance to carry these fearful remains about with me, with the thought that some of them might have belonged to him whom I have murdered. Therefore I sought for them round about, in the deep beds of the mountain-torrents, and in the high nests of the eagles and vultures. And while I was searching, I sometimes—could it have been only an illusion?—seemed to meet a being who was very like myself, but far, far more powerful, and yet still paler and more haggard."

An imploring look from Sintram stopped the flow of his words. With a gentle smile, Weigand bowed towards him, and said: "You know now all the deep, unutterably deep, sorrow which preyed upon me. My fear of you, and my yearning love for you, are no longer an enigma to your kind heart. For, dear youth, though you may be like your fearful father, you have also the kind, gentle heart of your mother; and its reflection brightens your pallid, stern features, like the glow of a morning sky, which lights up ice-covered mountains and snowy valleys with the soft radiance of joy. But, alas! how long you have lived alone amidst your fellow-creatures! and how long since you have seen your mother, my dearly-loved Sintram!"

"I feel, too, as though a spring were gushing up in the barren wilderness," replied the youth; "and I should perchance be altogether restored, could I but keep you long with me, and weep with you, dear lord. But I have that within me which says that you will very soon be taken from me."

"I believe, indeed," said the pilgrim, "that my late song was very nearly my last, and that it contained a prediction full soon to be accomplished in me. But, as the soul of man is always like the thirsty ground, the more blessings God has bestowed on us, the more earnestly do we look out for new ones; so would I crave for one more before, as I hope, my blessed end. Yet, indeed, it cannot be granted me," added he, with a faltering voice; "for I feel myself too utterly unworthy of so high a gift."

"But it will be granted!" said the chaplain, joyfully. "'He that humbleth himself shall be exalted;' and I fear not to take one purified from murder to receive a farewell from the holy and forgiving countenance of Verena."

The pilgrim stretched both his hands up towards heaven and an unspoken thanksgiving poured from his beaming eyes, and brightened the smile that played on his lips.

Sintram looked sorrowfully on the ground, and sighed gently to himself: "Alas! who would dare accompany?"

"My poor, good Sintram," said the chaplain, in a tone of the softest kindness, "I understand thee well; but the time is not yet come. The powers of evil will again raise up their wrathful heads within thee, and Verena must check both her own and thy longing desires, until all is pure in thy spirit as in hers. Comfort thyself with the thought that God looks mercifully upon thee, and that the joy so earnestly sought for will come—if not here, most assuredly beyond the grave."

But the pilgrim, as though awaking out of a trance, rose mightily from his seat, and said: "Do you please to come forth with me, reverend chaplain? Before the sun appears in the heavens, we could reach the convent-gates, and I should not be far from heaven."

In vain did the chaplain and Rolf remind him of his weakness: he smiled, and said that there could be no words about it; and he girded himself, and tuned the lute which he had asked leave to take with him. His decided manner overcame all opposition, almost without words; and the chaplain had already prepared himself for the journey, when the pilgrim looked with much emotion at Sintram, who, oppressed with a strange weariness, had sunk, half-asleep, on a couch, and said: "Wait a moment. I know that he wants me to give him a soft lullaby." The pleased smile of the youth seemed to say, Yes; and the pilgrim, touching the strings with a light hand, sang these words:

"Sleep peacefully, dear boy;
Thy mother sends the song
That whispers round thy couch,
To lull thee all night long.
In silence and afar
For thee she ever prays,
And longs once more in fondness
Upon thy face to gaze.

And when thy waking cometh,
Then in thy every deed,
In all that may betide thee,
Unto her words give heed.
Oh, listen for her voice,
If it be yea or nay;
And though temptation meet thee,
Thou shalt not miss the way.

If thou canst listen rightly,
And nobly onward go,
Then pure and gentle breezes
Around thy cheek shall blow.
Then on thy peaceful journey
Her blessing thou shalt feel,
And though from thee divided,
Her presence o'er thee steal.

O safest, sweetest comfort!
O blest and living light!
That, strong in Heaven's power,

All terrors put to flight!
Rest quietly, sweet child,
And may the gentle numbers
Thy mother sends to thee
Waft peace unto thy slumbers."

Sintram fell into a deep sleep, smiling, and breathing softly. Rolf and the castellan remained by his bed, whilst the two travellers pursued their way in the quiet starlight.

CHAPTER 22

The dawn had almost appeared, when Rolf, who had been asleep, was awakened by low singing; and as he looked round, he perceived, with surprise, that the sounds came from the lips of the castellan, who said, as if in explanation, "So does Sir Weigand sing at the convent- gates, and they are kindly opened to him." Upon which, old Rolf fell asleep again, uncertain whether what had passed had been a dream or a reality. After a while the bright sunshine awoke him again; and when he rose up, he saw the countenance of the castellan wonderfully illuminated by the red morning rays; and altogether those features, once so fearful, were shining with a soft, nay almost child-like mildness. The mysterious man seemed to be the while listening to the motionless air, as if he were hearing a most pleasant discourse or lofty music; and as Rolf was about to speak, he made him a sign of entreaty to remain quiet, and continued in his eager listening attitude.

At length he sank slowly and contentedly back in his seat, whispering, "God be praised! She has granted his last prayer; he will be laid in the burial- ground of the convent, and now he has forgiven me in the depths of his heart. I can assure you that he finds a peaceful end."

Rolf did not dare ask a question, or awake his lord; he felt as if one already departed had spoken to him.

The castellan long remained still, always smiling brightly. At last he raised himself a little, again listened, and said, "It is over. The sound of the bells is very sweet. We have overcome. Oh, how soft and easy does the good God make it to us!" And so it came to pass. He stretched himself back as if weary, and his soul was freed from his care-worn body.

Rolf now gently awoke his young knight, and pointed to the smiling dead. And Sintram smiled too; he and his good esquire fell on their knees, and prayed to God for the departed spirit. Then they rose up, and bore the cold body to the vaulted hall, and watched by it with holy candles until the return of the chaplain. That the pilgrim would not come back again, they very well knew.

Accordingly towards mid-day the chaplain returned alone. He could scarcely do more than confirm what was already known to them. He only added a comforting and hopeful greeting from Sintram's mother to her son, and told that the blissful Weigand had fallen asleep like a tired child, whilst Verena, with calm tenderness, held a crucifix before him.

"And in eternal peace our penance end!"

sang Sintram, gently to himself: and they prepared a last resting place for the now peaceful castellan, and laid him therein with all the due solemn rites.

The chaplain was obliged soon afterwards to depart; but bidding Sintram farewell, he again said kindly to him, "Thy dear mother assuredly knows how gentle and calm and good thou art now!"

CHAPTER 23

In the castle of Sir Biorn of the Fiery Eyes, Christmas-eve had not passed so brightly and happily; but yet, there too all had gone visibly according to God's will.

Folko, at the entreaty of the lord of the castle, had allowed Gabrielle to support him into the hall; and the three now sat at the round stone table, whereon a sumptuous meal was laid. On either side there were long tables, at which sat the retainers of both knights in full armour, according to the custom of the North. Torches and lamps lighted the lofty hall with an almost dazzling brightness.

Midnight had now begun its solemn reign, and Gabrielle softly reminded her wounded knight to withdraw. Biorn heard her, and said: "You are right, fair lady; our knight needs rest. Only let us first keep up one more old honourable custom."

And at his sign four attendants brought in with pomp a great boar's head, which looked as if cut out of solid gold, and placed it in the middle of the stone table. Biorn's retainers rose with reverence, and took off their helmets; Biorn himself did the same.

"What means this?" asked Folko very gravely.

"What thy forefathers and mine have done on every Yule feast," answered Biorn. "We are going to make vows on the boar's head, and then pass the goblet round to their fulfilment."

"We no longer keep what our ancestors called the Yule feast," said Folko; "we are good Christians, and we keep holy Christmas-tide."

"To do the one, and not to leave the other undone," answered Biorn. "I hold my ancestors too dear to forget their knightly customs. Those who think otherwise may act according to their wisdom, but that shall not hinder me. I swear by the golden boar's head—" And he stretched out his hand, to lay it solemnly upon it.

But Folko called out, "In the name of our holy Saviour, forbear. Where I am, and still have breath and will, none shall celebrate undisturbed the rites of the wild heathens."

Biorn of the Fiery Eyes glared angrily at him. The men of the two barons separated from each other, with a hollow sound of rattling armour, and ranged themselves in two bodies on either side of the hall, each behind its leader. Already here and there helmets were fastened and visors closed.

"Bethink thee yet what thou art doing," said Biorn. "I was about to vow an eternal union with the house of Montfaucon, nay, even to bind myself to do it grateful homage; but if thou disturb me in the customs which have come to me from my forefathers, look to thy safety and the safety of all that is dear to thee. My wrath no longer knows any bounds."

Folko made a sign to the pale Gabrielle to retire behind his followers, saying to her, "Be of good cheer, my noble wife, weaker Christians have braved, for the sake of God and of His holy Church, greater dangers than now seem to threaten us. Believe me, the Lord of Montfaucon is not so easily ensnared."

Gabrielle obeyed, something comforted by Folko's fearless smile, but this smile inflamed yet more the fury of Biorn. He again stretched out his hand towards the boar's head, as if about to make some dreadful vow, when Folko snatched a gauntlet of Biorn's off the table, with which he, with his unwounded left arm, struck so powerful a blow on the gilt idol, that it fell crashing to the ground, shivered to pieces. Biorn and his followers stood as if turned to stone. But soon swords were grasped by armed hands, shields were taken down from the walls, and an angry, threatening murmur sounded through the hall.

At a sign from Folko, a battle-axe was brought him by one of his faithful retainers; he swung it high in air with his powerful left hand, and stood looking like an avenging angel as he spoke these words through the tumult with awful calmness: "What seek ye, O deluded Northman? What wouldst thou, sinful lord? Ye are indeed become heathens; and I hope to show you, by my readiness for battle, that it is not in my right arm alone that God has put strength for victory. But if ye can yet hear, listen to my words. Biorn, on this same accursed, and now, by God's help, shivered boar's head, thou didst lay thy hand when thou didst swear to sacrifice any inhabitants of the German towns that should fall into thy power. And Gotthard Lenz came, and Rudlieb came, driven on these shores by the storm. What didst thou then do, O savage Biorn? What did ye do at his bidding, ye who were keeping the Yule feast with him? Try your fortune on me. The Lord will be with me, as He was with those holy men. To arms, and—" (he turned to his warriors) "let our battle-cry be Gotthard and Rudlieb!"

Then Biorn let drop his drawn sword, then his followers paused, and none among the Norwegians dared lift his eyes from the ground. By degrees, they one by one began to disappear from the hall; and at last Biorn stood quite alone opposite to the baron and his followers. He seemed hardly aware that he had been deserted, but he fell on his knees, stretched out his shining sword, pointed to the broken boar's head, and said, "Do with me as you have done with that; I deserve no better. I ask but one favour, only one; do not disgrace me, noble baron, by seeking shelter in another castle of Norway."

"I fear you not," answered Folko, after some thought; "and, as far as may be, I freely forgive you." Then he drew the sign of the cross over the wild form of Biorn, and left the hall with Gabrielle. The retainers of the house of Montfaucon followed him proudly and silently.

The hard spirit of the fierce lord of the castle was now quite broken, and he watched with increased humility every look of Folko and Gabrielle. But they withdrew more and more into the happy solitude of their own apartments, where they enjoyed, in the midst of the sharp winter, a bright spring-tide of happiness. The wounded condition of Folko did not hinder the evening delights of songs and music and poetry—but rather a new charm was added to them when the tall, handsome knight leant on the arm of his delicate lady, and they thus, changing as it were their deportment and duties, walked slowly through the torch-lit halls, scattering their kindly greetings like flowers among the crowds of men and women.

All this time little or nothing was heard of poor Sintram. The last wild outbreak of his father had increased the terror with which Gabrielle remembered the self-accusations of the youth; and the more resolutely Folko kept silence, the more did she bode some dreadful mystery. Indeed, a secret shudder came over the knight when he thought on the pale, dark-haired youth. Sintram's repentance had bordered on settled despair; no one knew even what he was doing in the fortress of evil report on the Rocks of the Moon. Strange rumours were brought by the retainers who had fled from it, that the evil spirit had obtained complete power over Sintram, that no man could stay with him, and that the fidelity of the dark mysterious castellan had cost him his life.

Folko could hardly drive away the fearful suspicion that the lonely young knight was become a wicked magician.

And perhaps, indeed, evil spirits did flit about the banished Sintram, but it was without his calling them up. In his dreams he often saw the wicked enchantress Venus, in her golden chariot drawn by winged cats, pass over the battlements of the stone fortress, and heard her say, mocking him, "Foolish Sintram, foolish Sintram! hadst thou but obeyed the little Master! Thou wouldst now be in Helen's arms, and the Rocks of the Moon would be called the Rocks of Love, and the stone fortress would be the garden of roses. Thou wouldst have lost thy pale face and dark hair,—for thou art only enchanted, dear youth,—and thine eyes would have beamed more softly, and thy cheeks bloomed more freshly, and thy hair would have been more golden than was that of Prince Paris when men wondered at his beauty. Oh, how Helen would have loved thee!" Then she showed him in a mirror, how, as a marvellously beautiful knight, he knelt before Gabrielle, who sank into his arms blushing as the morning. When he awoke from such dreams, he would seize eagerly the sword and scarf given him by his lady,—as a shipwrecked man seizes the plank which is to save him; and while the hot tears fell on them, he would murmur to himself, "There was, indeed, one hour in my sad life when I was worthy and happy."

Once he sprang up at midnight after one of these dreams, but this time with more thrilling horror; for it had seemed to him that the features of the enchantress Venus had changed towards the end of her speech, as she looked down upon him with marvellous scorn, and she appeared to him as the hideous little Master. The youth had no better means of calming his distracted mind than to throw the sword and scarf of Gabrielle over his shoulders, and to hasten forth under the solemn starry canopy of the wintry sky. He walked in deep thought backwards and forwards under the leafless oaks and the snow- laden firs which grew on the high ramparts.

Then he heard a sorrowful cry of distress sound from the moat; it was as if some one were attempting to sing, but was stopped by inward grief. Sintram exclaimed, "Who's there?" and all was still. When he was silent, and again began his walk, the frightful groanings and moanings were heard afresh, as if they came from a dying person. Sintram overcame the horror which seemed to hold him back, and began in silence to climb down into the deep dry moat which was cut in the rock. He was soon so low down that he could no longer see the stars shining; beneath him moved a shrouded form; and sliding with involuntary haste down the steep descent, he stood near the groaning figure; it ceased its lamentations, and began to laugh like a maniac from beneath its long, folded, female garments.

"Oh ho, my comrade! oh ho, my comrade! wert thou going a little too fast? Well, well, it is all right; and see now, thou standest no higher than I, my pious, valiant youth! Take it patiently,—take it patiently!"

"What dost thou want with me? Why dost thou laugh? why dost thou weep?" asked Sintram impatiently.

"I might ask thee the same questions," answered the dark figure, "and thou wouldst be less able to answer me than I to answer thee. Why dost thou laugh? why dost thou weep?—Poor creature! But I will show thee a remarkable thing in thy fortress, of which thou knowest nothing. Give heed!"

And the shrouded figure began to scratch and scrape at the stones till a little iron door opened, and showed a long passage which led into the deep darkness.

"Wilt thou come with me?" whispered the strange being; "it is the shortest way to thy father's castle. In half-an-hour we shall come out of this passage, and we shall be in thy beauteous lady's apartment. Duke Menelaus shall lie in a magic sleep,—leave that to me,—and then thou wilt take the slight, delicate form in thine arms, and bring her to the Rocks of the Moon; so thou wilt win back all that seemed lost by thy former wavering."

Sintram trembled visibly, fearfully shaken to and fro by the fever of passion and the stings of conscience. But at last, pressing the sword and scarf to his heart, he cried out, "Oh! that fairest, most glorious hour of my life! If I lose all other joys, I will hold fast that brightest hour!"

"A bright, glorious hour!" said the figure from under its veil, like an evil echo. "Dost thou know whom thou then conqueredst? A good old friend, who only showed himself so sturdy to give thee the glory of overcoming him. Wilt thou convince thyself? Wilt thou look?"

The dark garments of the little figure flew open, and the dwarf warrior in strange armour, the gold horns on his helmet, and the curved spear in his hand, the very same whom Sintram thought he had slain on Niflung's Heath, now stood before him and laughed: "Thou seest, my youth, everything in the wide world is but dreams and froth; wherefore hold fast the dream which delights thee, and sip up the froth which refreshes thee! Hasten to that underground passage, it leads up to thy angel Helen. Or wouldst thou first know thy friend yet better?"

His visor opened, and the hateful face of the little Master glared upon the knight. Sintram asked, as if in a dream, "Art thou also that wicked enchantress Venus?"

"Something like her," answered the little Master, laughing, "or rather she is something like me. And if thou wilt only get disenchanted, and recover the beauty of Prince of Paris,—then, O Prince Paris," and his voice changed to an alluring song, "then, O Prince Paris, I shall be fair like thee!"

At this moment the good Rolf appeared above on the rampart; a consecrated taper in his lantern shone down into the moat, as he sought for the missing young knight. "In God's name, Sir Sintram," he called out, "what has the spectre of whom you slew on Niflung's Heath, and whom I never could bury, to do with you?"

"Seest thou well? hearest thou well?" whispered the little Master, and drew back into the darkness of the underground passage. "The wise man up there knows me well. There was nothing in thy heroic feat. Come, take the joys of life while thou mayst."

But Sintram sprang back, with a strong effort, into the circle of light made by the shining of the taper from above, and cried out, "Depart from me, unquiet spirit! I know well that I bear a name on me in which thou canst have no part."

Little Master rushed in fear and rage into the passage, and, yelling, shut the iron door behind him. It seemed as if he could still be heard groaning and roaring.

Sintram climbed up the wall of the moat, and made a sign to his foster-father not to speak to him: he only said, "One of my best joys, yes, the very best, has been taken from me; but, by God's help, I am not yet lost."

In the earliest light of the following morning, he and Rolf stopped up the entrance to the perilous passage with huge blocks of stone.

CHAPTER 24

The long northern winter was at last ended, the fresh green leaves rustled merrily in the woods, patches of soft moss twinkled amongst the rocks, the valleys grew green, the brooks sparkled, the snow melted from all but the highest mountain-tops, and the bark which was ready to carry away Folko and Gabrielle danced on the sunny waves of the sea. The baron, now quite recovered, and strong and fresh as though his health had sustained no injury, stood one morning on the shore with his fair lady; and, full of glee at the prospect of returning to their home, the noble pair looked on well pleased at their attendants who were busied in lading the ship.

Then said one of them in the midst of a confused sound of talking: "But what has appeared to me the most fearful and the most strange thing in this northern land is the stone fortress on the Rocks of the Moon: I have never, indeed, been inside it, but when I used to see it in our huntings, towering above the tall fir-trees, there came a tightness over my breast, as if something unearthly were dwelling in it. And a few weeks ago, when the snow was yet lying hard in the valleys, I came unawares quite close upon the strange building. The young knight Sintram was walking alone on the ramparts as twilight came on, like the spirit of a departed knight, and he drew from the lute which he carried such soft, melancholy tones, and he sighed so deeply and sorrowfully... ."

The voice of the speaker was drowned in the noise of the crowd, and as he also just then reached the ship with his package hastily fastened up, Folko and Gabrielle could not hear the rest of his speech. But the fair lady looked on her knight with eyes dim with tears, and sighed: "Is it not behind those mountains that the Rocks of the Moon lie? The unhappy Sintram makes me sad at heart."

"I understand thee, sweet gracious lady, and the pure compassion of thy heart," replied Folko; instantly ordering his swift-footed steed to be brought. He placed his noble lady under the charge of his retainers, and leaping into the saddle, he hastened, followed by the grateful smiles of Gabrielle, along the valley towards the stone fortress.

Sintram was seated near the drawbridge, touching the strings of the lute, and shedding some tears on the golden chords, almost as Montfaucon's esquire had described him. Suddenly a cloudy shadow passed over him, and he looked up, expecting to see a flight of cranes in the air; but the sky was clear and blue. While the young knight was still wondering, a long bright spear fell at his feet from a battlement of the armoury turret.

"Take it up,—make good use of it! thy foe is near at hand! Near also is the downfall of thy dearest happiness." Thus he heard it distinctly whispered in his ear; and it seemed to him that he saw the shadow of the little Master glide close by him to a neighbouring cleft in the rock. But at the same time also, a tall, gigantic, haggard figure passed along the valley, in some measure like the departed pilgrim, only much, very much, larger, and he raised his long bony arm fearfully threatening, then disappeared in an ancient tomb.

At the very same instant Sir Folko of Montfaucon came swiftly as the wind up the Rocks of the Moon, and he must have seen something of those strange apparitions, for as he stopped close behind Sintram, he looked rather pale, and asked low and earnestly: "Sir knight, who are those two with whom you were just now holding converse here?"

"The good God knows," answered Sintram; "I know them not."

"If the good God does but know!" cried Montfaucon: "but I fear me that He knows very little more of you or your deeds."

"You speak strangely harsh words," said Sintram. "Yet ever since that evening of misery,—alas! and even long before,—I must bear with all that comes from you. Dear sir, you may believe me, I know not those fearful companions; I call them not, and I know not what terrible curse binds them to my footsteps. The merciful God, as I would hope, is mindful of me the while, —as a faithful shepherd does not forget even the worst and most widely-straying of his flock, but calls after it with an anxious voice in the gloomy wilderness."

Then the anger of the baron was quite melted. Two bright tears stood in his eyes, and he said: "No, assuredly, God has not forgotten thee; only do thou not forget thy gracious God. I did not come to rebuke thee—I came to bless thee in Gabrielle's name and in my own. The Lord preserve thee, the Lord guide thee, the Lord lift thee up! And, Sintram, on the far-off shores of Normandy I shall bear thee in mind, and I shall hear how thou strugglest against the curse which weighs down thy unhappy life; and if thou ever shake it off, and stand as a noble conqueror over Sin and Death, then thou shalt receive from me a token of love and reward, more precious then either thou or I can understand at this moment."

The words flowed prophetically from the baron's lips; he himself was only half-conscious of what he said. With a kind salutation he turned his noble steed, and again flew down the valley towards the sea-shore.

"Fool, fool! thrice a fool!" whispered the angry voice of the little Master in Sintram's ear. But old Rolf was singing his morning hymn in clear tones within the castle, and the last lines were these:—

"Whom worldlings scorn,
Who lives forlorn,
On God's own word doth rest;
With heavenly light
His path is bright,
His lot among the blest."

Then a holy joy took possession of Sintram's heart, and he looked around him yet more gladly than in the hour when Gabrielle gave him the scarf and sword, and Folko dubbed him knight.

CHAPTER 25

The baron and his lovely lady were sailing across the broad sea with favouring gales of spring, nay the coast of Normandy had already appeared above the waves; but still was Biorn of the Fiery Eye sitting gloomy and speechless in his castle. He had taken no leave of his guests. There was more of proud fear of Montfaucon than of reverential love for him in his soul, especially since the adventure with the boar's head; and the thought was bitter to his haughty spirit, that the great baron, the flower and glory of their whole race, should have come in peace to visit him, and should now be departing in displeasure, in stern reproachful displeasure. He had it constantly before his mind, and it never failed to bring fresh pangs, the remembrance of how all had come to pass, and how all might have gone otherwise; and he was always fancying he could hear the songs in which after generations would recount this voyage of the great Folko, and the worthlessness of the savage Biorn. At length, full of fierce anger, he cast away the fetters of his troubled spirit, he burst out of the castle with all his horsemen, and began to carry on a warfare more fearful and more lawless than any in which he had yet been engaged.

Sintram heard the sound of his father's war-horn; and committing the stone fortress to old Rolf, he sprang forth ready armed for the combat. But the flames of the cottages and farms on the mountains rose up before him, and showed him, written as if in characters of fire, what kind of war his father was waging. Yet he went on towards the spot where the army was mustered, but only to offer his mediation, affirming that he would not lay his hand on his good sword in so abhorred a service, even though the stone fortress, and his father's castle besides, should fall before the vengeance of their enemies. Biorn hurled the spear which he held in his hand against his son with mad fury. The deadly weapon whizzed past him: Sintram remained standing with his visor raised, he did not move one limb in his defence, when he said: "Father, do what you will; but I join not in your godless warfare."

Biorn of the Fiery Eyes laughed scornfully: "It seems I am always to have a spy over me here; my son succeeds to the dainty French knight!" But nevertheless he came to himself, accepted Sintram's mediation, made amends for the injuries he had done, and returned gloomily to his castle. Sintram went back to the Rocks of the Moon.

Such occurrences were frequent after that time. It went so far that Sintram came to be looked upon as the protector of all those whom his father pursued with relentless fury; but nevertheless sometimes his own wildness would carry the young knight away to accompany his fierce father in his fearful deeds. Then Biorn used to laugh with horrible pleasure, and to say: "See there, my son, how the flames we have lighted blaze up from the villages, as the blood spouts up from the wounds our swords have made! It is plain to me, however much thou mayst pretend to the contrary, that thou art, and wilt ever remain, my true and beloved heir!"

After thus fearfully erring, Sintram could find no comfort but in hastening to the chaplain of Drontheim, and confessing to him his misery and his sins. The chaplain would freely absolve him, after due penance and repentance, and again raise up the broken-hearted youth; but would often say: "Oh, how nearly hadst thou reached thy last trial, and gained the victory, and looked on Verena's countenance, and atoned for all! Now thou hast thrown thyself back for years. Think, my son, on the shortness of man's life; if thou art always falling back anew, how wilt thou ever gain the summit on this side the grave?"

*** *** ***

Years came and went, and Biorn's hair was white as snow, and the youth Sintram had reached the middle age. Old Rolf was now scarcely able to leave the stone fortress; and sometimes he said: "I feel it a burden that my life should yet be prolonged; but also there is much comfort in it, for I still think the good God has in store for me here below some great happiness; and it must be something in which you are concerned, my beloved Sir Sintram, for what else in the whole world could rejoice me?"

But all remained as it was, and Sintram's fearful dreams at Christmas-time each year rather increased than diminished in horror. Again the holy season was drawing near, and the mind of the sorely afflicted knight was more troubled than ever before. Sometimes, if he had been reckoning up the nights till it should come, a cold sweat would stand on his forehead, while he said, "Mark my words, dear old foster-father, this time something most awfully decisive lies before me."

One evening he felt an overwhelming anxiety about his father. It seemed to him that the Prince of Darkness was going up to Biorn's castle; and in vain did Rolf remind him that the snow was lying deep in the valleys, in vain did he suggest that the knight might be overtaken by his frightful dreams in the lonely mountains during the night-time. "Nothing can be worse to me than remaining here would be," replied Sintram.

He took his horse from the stable and rode forth in the gathering darkness. The noble steed slipped and stumbled and fell in the trackless way, but his rider always raised him up, and urged him only more swiftly and eagerly towards the object which he longed and yet dreaded to reach. Nevertheless he might never have arrived at it had not his faithful hound Skovmark kept with him. The dog sought out the lost track for his beloved master, and invited him into it with joyous barkings, and warned him by his howls against precipices and treacherous ice under the snow. Thus they arrived about midnight at Biorn's castle. The windows of the hall shone opposite to them with a brilliant light, as though some great feast were kept there, and confused sounds, as of singing, met their ears. Sintram gave his horse hastily to some retainers in the court-yard, and ran up the steps, whilst Skovmark stayed by the well-known horse.

A good esquire came towards Sintram within the castle and said, "God be praised, my dear master, that you are come; for surely nothing good is going on above. But take heed to yourself also, and be not deluded. Your father has a guest with him,—and, as I think—a hateful one."

Sintram shuddered as he threw open the doors. A little man in the dress of a miner was sitting with his back towards him. The armour had been for some time past again ranged round the stone table, so that only two places were left empty. The seat opposite the door had been taken by Biorn of the Fiery Eyes; and the dazzling light of the torches fell upon his features with so red a flare, that he perfectly enacted that fearful surname.

"Father, whom have you here with you?" cried Sintram; and his suspicions rose to certainty as the miner turned round, and the detestable face of the little Master grinned from under his dark hood.

"Yes, just see, my fair son," said the wild Biorn; "thou hast not been here for a long while,—and so to-night this jolly comrade has paid me a visit, and thy place has been taken. But throw one of the suits of armour out of the way, and put a seat for thyself instead of it,—and come and drink with us, and be merry."

"Yes, do so, Sir Sintram," said the little Master, with a laugh. "Nothing worse could come of it than that the broken pieces of armour might clatter somewhat strangely together, or at most that the disturbed spirit of him to whom the suit belonged might look over your shoulder; but he would not drink up any of our wine—ghosts have nothing to do with that. So now fall to!"

Biorn joined in the laughter of the hideous stranger with wild mirth; and while Sintram was mustering up his whole strength not to lose his senses at so terrible words, and was fixing a calm, steady look on the little Master's face, the old man cried out, "Why dost thou look at him so? Does it seem as though thou sawest thyself in a mirror? Now that you are together, I do not see it so much; but a while ago I thought that you were like enough to each other to be mistaken."

"God forbid!" said Sintram, walking up close to the fearful apparition: "I command thee, detestable stranger, to depart from this castle, in right of my authority as my father's heir,—as a consecrated knight and as a spirit!"

Biorn seemed as if he wished to oppose himself to this command with all his savage might. The little Master muttered to himself, "Thou art not by any means the master in this house, pious knight; thou hast never lighted a fire on this hearth." Then Sintram drew the sword which Gabrielle had given him, held the cross of the hilt before the eyes of his evil guest, and said, calmly, but with a powerful voice, "Worship or fly!" And he fled, the frightful stranger,— he fled with such lightning speed, that it could scarcely be seen whether he had sprung through the window or the door. But in going he overthrew some of the armour, the tapers went out, and it seemed that the pale blue flame which lighted up the whole in a marvellous manner gave a fulfilment to the little Master's former words: and that the spirits of those to whom the armour had belonged were leaning over the table, grinning fearfully.

Both the father and the son were filled with horror; but each chose an opposite way to save himself. Biorn wished to have his hateful guest back again; and the power of his will was seen when the little Master's step resounded anew on the stairs, and his brown shrivelled hand shook the lock of the door. On the other hand, Sintram ceased not to say within himself, "We are lost, if he come back! We are lost to all eternity, if he come back!" And he fell on his knees, and prayed fervently from his troubled heart to Father, Son, and Holy Ghost. Then the little Master left the door, and again Biorn willed him to return, and again Sintram's prayers drove him away. So went on this strife of wills throughout the long night; and howling whirlwinds raged the while around the castle, till all the household thought the end of the world was come.

At length the dawn of morning appeared through the windows of the hall, —the fury of the storm was lulled,—Biorn sank back powerless in slumber on his seat,—peace and hope came to the inmates of the castle,—and Sintram, pale and exhausted, went out to breathe the dewy air of the mild winter's morning before the castle-gates.

CHAPTER 26

The faithful Skovmark followed his master, caressing him; and when Sintram fell asleep on a stone seat in the wall, he lay at his feet, keeping watchful guard. Suddenly he pricked up his ears, looked round with delight, and bounded joyfully down the mountain. Just afterwards the chaplain of Drontheim appeared amongst the rocks, and the good beast went up to him as if to greet him, and then again ran back to the knight to announce the welcome visitor.

Sintram opened his eyes, as a child whose Christmas gifts have been placed at his bedside. For the chaplain smiled at him as he had never yet seen him smile. There was in it a token of victory and blessing, or at least of the near approach of both. "Thou hast done much yesterday, very much," said the holy priest; and his hands were joined, and his eyes full of bright tears. "I praise God for thee, my noble knight. Verena knows all, and she too praises God for thee. I do indeed now dare hope that the time will soon come when thou mayst appear before her. But Sintram, Sir Sintram, there is need of haste; for the old man above requires speedy air, and thou hast still a heavy—as I hope the last— yet a most heavy trial to undergo for his sake. Arm thyself, my knight, arm thyself even with bodily weapons. In truth, this time only spiritual armour is needed, but it always befits a knight, as well as a monk, to wear in decisive moments the entire solemn garb of his station. If it so please thee, we will go directly to Drontheim together. Thou must return thence to-night. Such is a part of the hidden decree, which has been dimly unfolded to Verena's foresight. Here there is yet much that is wild and distracting, and thou hast great need to-day of calm preparation."

With humble joy Sintram bowed his assent, and called for his horse and for a suit of armour. "Only," added he, "let not any of that armour be brought which was last night overthrown in the hall!"

His orders were quickly obeyed. The arms which were fetched, adorned with fine engraved work, the simple helmet, formed rather like that of an esquire than a knight, the lance of almost gigantic size, which belonged to the suit— on all these the chaplain gazed in deep thought and with melancholy emotion. At last, when Sintram, with the help of his esquires, was well-nigh equipped, the holy priest spoke:

"Wonderful providence of God! See, dear Sintram, this armour and this spear were formerly those of Sir Weigand the Slender, and with them he did many mighty deeds. When he was tended by your mother in the castle, and when even your father still showed himself kind towards him, he asked, as a favour, that his armour and his lance should be allowed to hang in Biorn's armoury—Weigand himself, as you well know, intended to build a cloister and to live there as a monk— and he put his old esquire's helmet with it, instead of another, because he was yet wearing that one when he first saw the fair Verena's angelic face. How wondrously does it now come to pass, that these very arms, which have so long been laid aside, should be brought to you for the decisive hour of your life! To me, as far as my short-sighted human wisdom can tell,—to me it seems truly a very solemn token, but one full of high and glorious promise."

Sintram stood now in complete array, composed and stately, and, from his tall slender figure, might have been taken for a youth, had not the deep lines of care which furrowed his countenance shown him to be advanced in years.

"Who has placed boughs on the head of my war-horse?" asked Sintram of the esquires, with displeasure. "I am not a conqueror, nor a wedding-guest. And besides, there are no boughs now but those red and yellow crackling oak-leaves, dull and dead like the season itself."

"Sir Knight, I know not myself," answered an esquire; "but it seemed to me that it must be so."

"Let it be," said the chaplain. "I feel that this also comes as a token full of meaning from the right source."

Then the knight threw himself into his saddle; the priest went beside him; and they both rode slowly and silently towards Drontheim. The faithful dog followed his master. When the lofty castle of Drontheim appeared in sight, a gentle smile spread itself over Sintram's countenance, like sunshine over a wintry valley. "God has done great things for me," said he. "I once rushed from here, a fearfully wild boy; I now come back a penitent man. I trust that it will yet go well with my poor troubled life."

The chaplain assented kindly, and soon afterwards the travellers passed under the echoing vaulted gateway into the castle-yard. At a sign from the priest, the retainers approached with respectful haste, and took charge of the horse; then he and Sintram went through long winding passages and up many steps to the remote chamber which the chaplain had chosen for himself; far away from the noise of men, and near to the clouds and the stars. There the two passed a quiet day in devout prayer, and earnest reading of Holy Scripture.

When the evening began to close in, the chaplain arose and said: "And now, my knight, get ready thy horse, and mount and ride back again to thy father's castle. A toilsome way lies before thee, and I dare not go with you. But I can and will call upon the Lord for you all through the long fearful night. O beloved instrument of the Most High, thou wilt yet not be lost!"

Thrilling with strange forebodings, but nevertheless strong and vigorous in spirit, Sintram did according to the holy man's desire. The sun set as the knight approached a long valley, strangely shut in by rocks, through which lay the road to his father's castle.

CHAPTER 27

Before entering the rocky pass, the knight, with a prayer and thanksgiving, looked back once more at the castle of Drontheim. There it was, so vast and quiet and peaceful; the bright windows of the chaplain's high chamber yet lighted up by the last gleam of the sun, which had already disappeared. In front of Sintram was the gloomy valley, as if his grave. Then there came towards him some one riding on a small horse; and Skovmark, who had gone up to the stranger as if to find out who he was, now ran back with his tail between his legs and his ears put back, howling and whining, and crept, terrified, under his master's war-horse. But even the noble steed appeared to have forgotten his once so fearless and warlike ardour. He trembled violently, and when the knight would have turned him towards the stranger, he reared and snorted and plunged, and began to throw himself backwards. It was only with difficulty that Sintram's strength and horsemanship got the better of him; and he was all white with foam when Sintram came up to the unknown traveller.

"You have cowardly beasts with you," said the latter, in a low, smothered voice.

Sintram was unable, in the ever-increasing darkness, rightly to distinguish what kind of being he saw before him; only a very pallid face, which at first he had thought was covered with freshly fallen snow, met his eyes from amidst the long hanging garments. It seemed that the stranger carried a small box wrapped up; his little horse, as if wearied out, bent his head down towards the ground, whereby a bell, which hung from the wretched torn bridle under his neck, was made to give a strange sound. After a short silence, Sintram replied: "Noble steeds avoid those of a worse race, because they are ashamed of them; and the boldest dogs are attacked by a secret terror at sight of forms to which they are not accustomed. I have no cowardly beasts with me."

"Good, sir knight; then ride with me through the valley."

"I am going through the valley, but I want no companions."

"But perhaps I want one. Do you not see that I am unarmed? And at this season, at this hour, there are frightful, unearthly beasts about."

Just then, as though to confirm the awful words of the stranger, a thing swung itself down from one of the nearest trees, covered with hoar-frost,—no one could say if it were a snake or a lizard,—it curled and twisted itself, and appeared about to slide down upon the knight or his companion. Sintram levelled his spear, and pierced the creature through. But, with the most hideous contortions, it fixed itself firmly on the spear-head; and in vain did the knight endeavour to rub it off against the rocks or the trees. Then he let his spear rest upon his right shoulder, with the point behind him, so that the horrible beast no longer met his sight; and he said, with good courage, to the stranger, "It does seem, indeed, that I could help you, and I am not forbidden to have an unknown stranger in my company; so let us push on bravely into the valley!"

"Help!" so resounded the solemn answer; "not help. I perhaps may help thee. But God have mercy upon thee if the time should ever come when I could no longer help thee. Then thou wouldst be lost, and I should become very frightful to thee. But we will go through the valley—I have thy knightly word for it. Come!"

They rode forward; Sintram's horse still showing signs of fear, the faithful dog still whining; but both obedient to their master's will. The knight was calm and steadfast. The snow had slipped down from the smooth rocks, and by the light of the rising moon could be seen various strange twisted shapes on their sides, some looking like snakes, and some like human faces; but they were only formed by the veins in the rock and the half-bare roots of trees, which had planted themselves in that desert place with capricious firmness. High above, and at a great distance, the castle of Drontheim, as if to take leave, appeared again through an opening in the rocks. The knight then looked keenly at his companion, and he almost felt as if Weigand the Slender were riding beside him.

"In God's name," cried he, "art thou not the shade of that departed knight who suffered and died for Verena?"

"I have not suffered, I have not died; but ye suffer, and ye die, poor mortals!" murmured the stranger. "I am not Weigand. I am that other, who was so like him, and whom thou hast also met before now in the wood."

Sintram strove to free himself from the terror which came over him at these words. He looked at his horse; it appeared to him entirely altered. The dry, many-coloured oak-leaves on its head were waving like the flames around a sacrifice, in the uncertain moonlight. He looked down again, to see after his faithful Skovmark. Fear had likewise most wondrously changed him. On the ground in the middle of the road were lying dead men's bones, and hideous lizards were crawling about; and, in defiance of the wintry season, poisonous mushrooms were growing up all around.

"Can this be still my horse on which I am riding?" said the knight to himself, in a low voice; "and can that trembling beast which runs at my side be my dog?"

Then some one called after him, in a yelling voice, "Stop! stop! Take me also with you!"

Looking round, Sintram perceived a small, frightful figure with horns, and a face partly like a wild boar and partly like a bear, walking along on its hind-legs, which were those of a horse; and in its hand was a strange, hideous weapon, shaped like a hook or a sickle. It was the being who had been wont to trouble him in his dreams; and, alas! it was also the wretched little Master himself, who, laughing wildly, stretched out a long claw towards the knight.

The bewildered Sintram murmured, "I must have fallen asleep; and now my dreams are coming over me!"

"Thou art awake," replied the rider of the little horse, "but thou knowest me also in thy dreams. For, behold! I am Death." And his garments fell from him, and there appeared a mouldering skeleton, its ghastly head crowned with serpents; that which he had kept hidden under his mantle was an hour-glass with the sand almost run out. Death held it towards the knight in his fleshless hand. The bell at the neck of the little horse gave forth a solemn sound. It was a passing bell.

"Lord, into Thy hands I commend my spirit!" prayed Sintram; and full of earnest devotion he rode after Death, who beckoned him on.

"He has thee not yet! He has thee not yet!" screamed the fearful fiend. "Give thyself up to me rather. In one instant,—for swift are thy thoughts, swift is my might,—in one instant thou shalt be in Normandy. Helen yet blooms in beauty as when she departed hence, and this very night she would be thine." And once again he began his unholy praises of Gabrielle's loveliness, and Sintram's heart glowed like wild-fire in his weak breast.

Death said nothing more, but raised the hour-glass in his right hand yet higher and higher; and as the sand now ran out more quickly, a soft light streamed from the glass over Sintram's countenance, and then it seemed to him as if eternity in all its calm majesty were rising before him, and a world of confusion dragging him back with a deadly grasp.

"I command thee, wild form that followest me," cried he, "I command thee, in the name of our Lord Jesus Christ, to cease from thy seducing words, and to call thyself by that name by which thou art recorded in Holy Writ!"

A name, more fearful than a thunderclap, burst despairingly from the lips of the Tempter, and he disappeared.

"He will return no more," said Death, in a kindly tone.

"And now I am become wholly thine, my stern companion?"

"Not yet, my Sintram. I shall not come to thee till many, many years are past. But thou must not forget me the while."

"I will keep the thought of thee steadily before my soul, thou fearful yet wholesome monitor, thou awful yet loving guide!"

"Oh! I can truly appear very gentle."

And so it proved indeed. His form became more softly defined in the increasing gleam of light which shone from the hour-glass; the features, which had been awful in their sternness, wore a gentle smile; the crown of serpents became a bright palm-wreath; instead of the horse appeared a white misty cloud in the moonlight; and the bell gave forth sounds as of sweet lullabies. Sintram thought he could hear these words amidst them:

"The world and Satan are o'ercome,
Before thee gleams eternal light,
Warrior, who hast won the strife:
Save from darkest shades of night
Him before whose aged eyes
All my terrors soon shall rise."

The knight well knew that his father was meant; and he urged on his noble steed, which now obeyed his master willingly and gladly, and the faithful dog also again ran beside him fearlessly. Death had disappeared; but in front of Sintram there floated a bright morning cloud, which continued visible after the sun had risen clear and warm in the bright winter sky.

CHAPTER 28

"He is dead! the horrors of that fearful stormy night have killed him!" Thus said, about this time, some of Biorn's retainers, who had not been able to bring him back to his senses since the morning of the day before: they had made a couch of wolf and bear skins for him in the great hall, in the midst of the armour which still lay scattered around. One of the esquires said with a low sigh: "The Lord have mercy on his poor wild soul!"

Just then the warder blew his horn from his tower, and a trooper came into the room with a look of surprise. "A knight is coming hither," said he; "a wonderful knight. I could have taken him for our Lord Sintram—but a bright, bright morning cloud floats so close before him, and throws over him such a clear light, that one could fancy red flowers were showered down upon him. Besides, his horse has a wreath of red leaves on his head, which was never a custom of the son of our dead lord."

"Just such a one," replied another, "I wove for him yesterday. He was not pleased with it at first, but afterwards he let it remain."

"But why didst thou that?"

"It seemed to me as if I heard a voice singing again and again in my ear: 'Victory! victory! the noblest victory! The knight rides forth to victory!' And then I saw a branch of our oldest oak-tree stretched towards me, which had kept on almost all its red and yellow leaves in spite of the snow. So I did according to what I had heard sung; and I plucked some of the leaves, and wove a triumphal wreath for the noble war-horse. At the same time Skovmark,—you know that the faithful beast had always a great dislike to Biorn, and therefore had gone to the stable with the horse,—Skovmark jumped upon me, fawning, and seemed pleased, as if he wanted to thank me for my work; and such noble animals understand well about good prognostics."

They heard the sound of Sintram's spurs on the stone steps, and Skovmark's joyous bark. At that instant the supposed corpse of old Biorn sat up, looked around with rolling, staring eyes, and asked of the terrified retainers in a hollow voice, "Who comes there, ye people? who comes there? I know it is my son. But who comes with him? The answer to that bears the sword of decision in its mouth. For see, good people, Gotthard and Rudlieb have prayed much for me; yet if the little Master come with him, I am lost in spite of them."

"Thou art not lost, my beloved father!" Sintram's kind voice was heard to say, as he softly opened the door, and the bright red morning cloud floated in with him.

Biorn joined his hands, cast a look of thankfulness up to heaven, and said, smiling, "Yes, praised be God! it is the right companion! It is sweet gentle death!" And then he made a sign to his son to approach, saying, "Come here, my deliverer; come, blessed of the Lord, that I may relate to thee all that has passed within me."

As Sintram now sat close by his father's couch, all who were in the room perceived a remarkable and striking change. For old Biorn, whose whole countenance, and not his eyes alone, had been wont to have a fiery aspect, was now quite pale, almost like white marble; while, on the other hand, the cheeks of the once deadly pale Sintram glowed with a bright bloom like that of early youth. It was caused by the morning cloud which still shone upon him, whose presence in the room was rather felt than seen; but it produced a gentle thrill in every heart.

"See, my son," began the old man, softly and mildly, "I have lain for a long time in a death-like sleep, and have known nothing of what was going on around me; but within,—ah! within, I have known but too much! I thought that my soul would be destroyed by the eternal anguish; and yet again I felt, with much greater horror, that my soul was eternal like that anguish. Beloved son, thy cheeks that glowed so brightly are beginning to grow pale at my words. I refrain from more. But let me relate to you something more cheering. Far, far away, I could see a bright lofty church, where Gotthard and Rudlieb Lenz were kneeling and praying for me. Gotthard had grown very old, and looked almost like one of our mountains covered with snow, on which the sun, in the lovely evening hours, is shining; and Rudlieb was also an elderly man, but very vigorous and very strong; and they both, with all their strength and vigour, were calling upon God to aid me, their enemy. Then I heard a voice like that of an angel, saying, 'His son does the most for him! He must this night wrestle with death and with the fallen one! His victory will be victory, and his defeat will be defeat, for the old man and himself.' Thereupon I awoke; and I knew that all depended upon whom thou wouldst bring with thee. Thou hast conquered. Next to God, the praise be to thee!"

"Gotthard and Rudlieb have helped much," replied Sintram; "and, beloved father, so have the fervent prayers of the chaplain of Drontheim. I felt, when struggling with temptation and deadly fear, how the heavenly breath of holy men floated round me and aided me."

"I am most willing to believe that, my noble son, and everything thou sayest to me," answered the old man; and at the same moment the chaplain also coming in, Biorn stretched out his hand towards him with a smile of peace and joy. And now all seemed to be surrounded with a bright circle of unity and blessedness. "But see," said old Biorn, "how the faithful Skovmark jumps upon me now, and tries to caress me. It is not long since he used always to howl with terror when he saw me."

"My dear lord," said the chaplain, "there is a spirit dwelling in good beasts, though dreamy and unconscious."

As the day wore on, the stillness in the hall increased. The last hour of the aged knight was drawing near, but he met it calmly and fearlessly. The chaplain and Sintram prayed beside his couch. The retainers knelt devoutly around. At length the dying man said: "Is that the prayer-bell in Verena's cloister?" Sintram's looks said yea; while warm tears fell on the colourless cheeks of his father. A gleam shone in the old man's eyes, the morning cloud stood close over him, and then the gleam, the morning cloud, and life with them, departed from him.

CHAPTER 29

A few days afterwards Sintram stood in the parlour of the convent, and waited with a beating heart for his mother to appear. He had seen her for the last time when, a slumbering child, he had been awakened by her warm farewell kisses, and then had fallen asleep again, to wonder in his dreams what his mother had wanted with him, and to seek her in vain the next morning in the castle and in the garden. The chaplain was now at his side, rejoicing in the chastened rapture of the knight, whose fierce spirit had been softened, on whose cheeks a light reflection of that solemn morning cloud yet lingered.

The inner doors opened. In her white veil, stately and noble, the Lady Verena came forward, and with a heavenly smile she beckoned her son to approach the grating. There could be no thought here of any passionate outbreak, whether of sorrow or of joy.

"In whose sweet presence sorrow dares not lower
Nor expectation rise
Too high for earth."—Christian Year.
(Footnote in 1901 text.)

The holy peace which had its abode within these walls would have found its way to a heart less tried and less purified than that which beat in Sintram's bosom. Shedding some placid tears, the son knelt before his mother, kissed her flowing garments through the grating, and felt as if in paradise, where every wish and every care is hushed. "Beloved mother," said he, "let me become a holy man, as thou art a holy woman. Then I will betake myself to the cloister yonder; and perhaps I might one day be deemed worthy to be thy confessor, if illness or the weakness of old age should keep the good chaplain within the castle of Drontheim."

"That would be a sweet, quietly happy life, my good child," replied the Lady Verena; "but such is not thy vocation. Thou must remain a bold, powerful knight, and thou must spend the long life, which is almost always granted to us children of the North, in succouring the weak, in keeping down the lawless, and in yet another more bright and honourable employment which I hitherto rather honour than know."

"God's will be done!" said the knight, and he rose up full of self- devotion and firmness.

"That is my good son," said the Lady Verena. "Ah! how many sweet calm joys spring up for us! See, already is our longing desire of meeting again satisfied, and thou wilt never more be so entirely estranged from me. Every week on this day thou wilt come back to me, and thou wilt relate what glorious deeds thou hast done, and take back with thee my advice and my blessing."

"Am I not once more a good and happy child!" cried Sintram joyously; "only that the merciful God has given me in addition the strength of a man in body and spirit. Oh, how blessed is that son to whom it is allowed to gladden his mother's heart with the blossoms and the fruit of his life!"

Thus he left the quiet cloister's shade, joyful in spirit and richly laden with blessings, to enter on his noble career. He was not content with going about wherever there might be a rightful cause to defend or evil to avert; the gates of the now hospitable castle stood always open also to receive and shelter every stranger; and old Rolf, who was almost grown young again at the sight of his lord's excellence, was established as seneschal. The winter of Sintram's life set in bright and glorious, and it was only at times that he would sigh within himself and say,

"Ah, Montfaucon! ah, Gabrielle! if I could dare to hope that you have quite forgiven me!"

CHAPTER 30

The spring had come in its brightness to the northern lands, when one morning Sintram turned his horse homewards, after a successful encounter with one of the most formidable disturbers of the peace of his neighbourhood. His horsemen rode after him, singing as they went. As they drew near the castle, they heard the sound of joyous notes wound on the horn. "Some welcome visitor must have arrived," said the knight; and he spurred his horse to a quicker pace over the dewy meadow. While still at some distance, they descried old Rolf, busily engaged in preparing a table for the morning meal, under the trees in front of the castle-gates. From all the turrets and battlements floated banners and flags in the fresh morning breeze: esquires were running to and fro in their gayest apparel. As soon as the good Rolf saw his master, he clapped his hands joyfully over his grey head, and hastened into the castle. Immediately the wide gates were thrown open; and Sintram, as he entered, was met by Rolf, whose eyes were filled with tears of joy while he pointed towards three noble forms that were following him.

Two men of high stature—one in extreme old age, the other grey-headed, and both remarkably alike—were leading between them a fair young boy, in a page's dress of blue velvet, richly embroidered with gold. The two old men wore the dark velvet dress of German burghers, and had massive gold chains and large shining medals hanging round their necks.

Sintram had never before seen his honoured guests, and yet he felt as if they were well known and valued friends. The very aged man reminded him of his dying father's words about the snow-covered mountains lighted up by the evening sun; and then he remembered, he could scarcely tell how, that he had heard Folko say that one of the highest mountains of that sort in his southern land was called the St. Gotthard. And at the same time, he knew that the old but yet vigorous man on the other side was named Rudlieb. But the boy who stood between them ah! Sintram's humility dared scarcely form a hope as to who he might be, however much his features, so noble and soft, called up two highly honoured images before his mind.

Then the aged Gotthard Lenz, the king of old men, advanced with a solemn step, and said—"This is the noble boy Engeltram of Montfaucon, the only son of the great baron; and his father and mother send him to you, Sir Sintram, knowing well your holy and glorious knightly career, that you may bring him up to all the honourable and valiant deeds of this northern land, and may make of him a Christian knight, like yourself."

Sintram threw himself from his horse. Engeltram of Montfaucon held the stirrup gracefully for him, checking the retainers, who pressed forward, with these words: "I am the noblest born esquire of this knight, and the service nearest to his person belongs to me."

Sintram knelt in silent prayer on the turf; then lifting up in his arms, towards the rising sun, the image of Folko and Gabrielle, he cried, "With the help of God, my Engeltram, thou wilt become glorious as that sun, and thy course will be like his!"

And old Rolf exclaimed, as he wept for joy, "Lord, now lettest Thou Thy servant depart in peace."

Gotthard Lenz and Rudlieb were pressed to Sintram's heart; the chaplain of Drontheim, who just then came from Verena's cloister to bring a joyful greeting to her brave son, stretched out his hands to bless them all.